Confessions of a Sandbagger

J.J. Gowland

PublishAmerica
Baltimore

© 2004 by J.J. Gowland.
All rights reserved. No part of this book may be reproduced, stored in a retrieval system or transmitted in any form or by any means without the prior written permission of the publishers, except by a reviewer who may quote brief passages in a review to be printed in a newspaper, magazine or journal.

First printing

ISBN: 1-4137-5527-5
PUBLISHED BY PUBLISHAMERICA, LLLP
www.publishamerica.com
Baltimore

Printed in the United States of America

Dedication

Dedicated to my grandparents, Walter and Mary Hayward, who gave me lessons in life, golf, business, and bequeathed ownership shares in golf courses in southern Ontario.

Acknowledgments

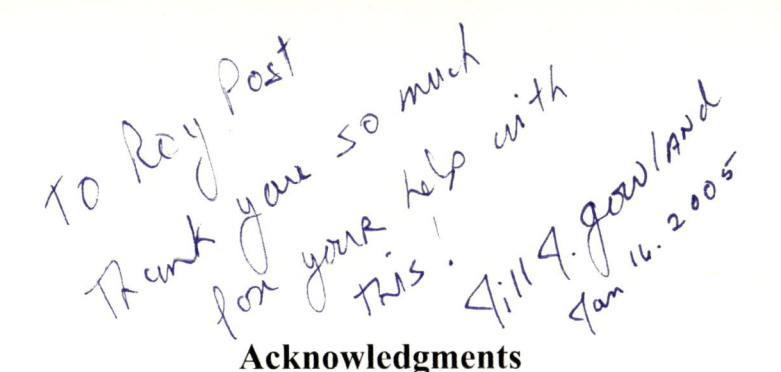

Special thanks go out to Susan McGuigan for being a great golfing partner, for being on the 17th tee when inspiration hit, for listening to story ideas, and for her editing advice.

I wish to thank the following: Bill Kovessy for the photographs of the 17th hole that kept the inspiration alive through the Canadian winter. Martha Watson for the photos of the beloved dog, Kaida. Brian Henry for all of his writing workshops. Paul Lacroix, a 25-year member of the CPGA, for confirming the golf tips found herein. Roy Post for his input about handling handicap mishaps. The Royal Canadian Golf Association and the USGA for the rules of golf and handicap information.

To junior golf programs everywhere, for lessons in more than just golf.

And last but not least, to Mom, who plays golf more than I do.

This is a work of fiction. Any resemblance to real people is purely coincidental, except the 17th hole is real.

Chapter 1

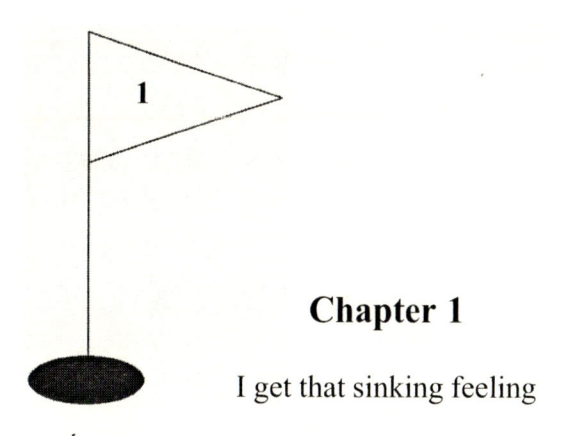

I get that sinking feeling

First of all, don't feel sorry for me. I've had a good life. I've done what I wanted to do. The fact that, as you read this, I am sinking into the pond on the 17th hole at CrossCreek Golf and Country Club shouldn't come as a surprise. I can honestly say it doesn't surprise me to find my life about to end in this way.

In one way, it's kind of ironic, if not downright symbolic. What better way for a sandbagger to approach his demise than with his body strapped to a golf bag stuffed with 15 clubs and old donated golf balls, and tossed into the pond on the signature hole of one of the most picturesque and perspicacious par-three golf holes in southern Ontario? I have to admire their creative revenge.

Did I mention that my pant legs are stuffed with at least three of those thin, blue plastic Toronto Star newspaper bags, all filled with sand, and my shirt and my pockets are stuffed with ziplock sandwich bags with more of the same kind of sand?

I don't know how many times I've stood on the 17th tee, par-three hole at CrossCreek and pondered, *How deep is that pond?* Over the years, as a member at CrossCreek, I pondered a number of other things as I stood there watching my non-betting opponents teeing off from the elevated tee, sending their balls to the green or fairway, and never scoring 'three off the tee' the way I could. I confess, I dumped my tee shot on the 17th hole into the pond more times than not, just to keep my handicap higher than it should be.

The par-three 17th hole at CrossCreek is a beauty. The tee is elevated, about fifty feet higher than the bunker-protected green. The green is a distance of one hundred and ninety yards from the championship tee, one hundred and seventy-one from the men's regular tee, one hundred and forty yards from the women's tee. There's a tree-shaded creek that runs behind the green to catch long shots. But about halfway between the tees and the green is a kidney shaped pond, with the green side bordered by bulrushes, and the surface dotted with pink, white, and rose coloured water lilies. In the spring, even from the tee, you can hear the song of the mating frogs, humming like a wheatfield full of crickets. It's a beautiful golf hole, and being the 17th hole, it draws on a player's stamina and focus, and psyches out some of the club's best players.

Normally, as I watch other players tee off, I calculate my score to that point and figure that if I manage a bogey or worse, my handicap will stay high. If I par the hole, my handicap might go down. If necessary, I'll manufacture a bad swing, pick the wrong club and pop up a fly ball to land smack dab in the middle of the pond. I essentially guarantee a bogey or worse. If I've had a bad round to that point, I'll focus, use the right club, and sail a shot as pretty as can be to the green for a two-putt par.

The rumoured title 'sandbagger' is not easy to maintain. As I sink into the depths of the pond, I can tell you, I worked very hard at keeping the dubious label. I remember every strategic shot, every planned move, every missed putt, every lousy sand shot, and every bet I ever won. I am meticulous with my records, sly with my giggles, and appropriately humbled when I, as a small loser, pay my hustler bets and dispute the description. Every now and then, a hustler has to payout, to keep the big losers coming back.

But also while I sink through the lily pads, I have to take credit for a number of improvements to the game. My life as a sandbagger has not totally been wasted and is seldom unrewarding. The guys really should thank me for making tournament golf a more honest game. The club wouldn't have instituted the art of tracking 'tournament' scores, and produced 'tournament' handicaps, if not for me and my style.

See, I'm a tournament player. I love tournaments, and always play my best.

Hours before the qualifying rounds of the club championship I'm dreaming of my course strategy, my putting stroke, my sand play, my approach shots. I visualise every shot, every hole, and every possible challenge. Three hours before tee-off, I'm mentally preparing for the game. Two hours before the tee-time, at home, I'm limbering up, stretching my muscles, practising my tempo, my alignment. Then, when I get to the course, I put on my 'oh well, I'm a sixteen handicapper. No way can I win' act. I don't let anyone see me stretch my muscles, check my tempo. I hit only half a dozen balls on the driving range, and most of them are bad shots. I make a show of putting on the practice green, but again, it's done for the audience, just to confirm that I'm going to miss most of my putts. I want the other players to think I'm a bozo on the course. Heh, heh. It's all part of my plan.

First tee jitters on tournament days are fun to watch. You'd think these guys had never learned the methods to diminish performance nervousness. I love the tension on the first tee as the guys line up, watch the foursome ahead, and individually pray that only he will do well. The way they act, you'd think they were consumed with stage fright.

Some are loud and boasting, some are quiet and unassuming, praying silently.

Some are going through routines, peeling Velcro on their golf glove, re-tying their shoes and cleaning spikes, checking golf and personal balls, adjusting underwear. It's a study in nervous habits. I like to arrive early at the club that day because the psychology of mannerisms is a free show. Better than the circus. Besides, being early gives me some time to arrange bets with the guys against whom, over beers in the clubhouse, I want to match scorecards.

I make a pocketful of dough on days like that. I love the jitters and nervousness these amateur golfers try to hide. Some of them have that glassy-eyed, 'deer-in-the-headlights' look even before they put on their golf shoes.

Because there were rumours that some guys were sandbaggers, the pro suggested keeping track of tournament scores, and calculating 'tournament' handicaps based on previous tournament scores. That could really screw me and my betting.

I am a tournament player. I played my best game in club tournaments, when side bet money or decent prizes were on the line. So, if I worked hard to keep my handicap up so that I could beat the pants off players in net score games, then the tournament scores and tournament handicaps would make my challenge even greater.

I learned that the cash sideline bets could give me a better pocketful of cash than the prizes on the table. If the top prize was a golf bag valued at $150 bucks, I'd make more in my 'match score card' bets. The prestige of winning the club championship was something a lot of guys aspired to, and winning does provide a few benefits, like reduced membership fees the next year, playing in the Southwestern Ontario Pro and Club Champions tournament, and your name on a trophy. But it couldn't buy that diamond tennis bracelet my wife wants or the sapphire earrings that my mistress sought after. Cash could do that and I collected more cash than you could shake a nine iron at.

I am a sandbagger and the reason those 'tournament' handicaps are in place. Blame me or thank me, it's not important now.

As I'm sinking in the pond on the 17th hole, it's only mid-morning, on one beautiful October Saturday, and every tee time is filled with a foursomes of golfers out for that one last day of golf before the snow falls. I still haven't finished playing the par-three and still had to play the 18th hole and maybe finish my best game of the season.

I glanced over to my right to watch for my playing partners, Jimmy, Ken, and Dan, to walk off the 18th tee and head up the fairway.

I called out, "Okay, guys! I get the picture. You want to haul me out of here now?"

Not even one of them turned to look at me.

Not one.

I know that the rest of the Saturday morning golfers spaced about ten minutes apart would be coming along to the 17th tee. Some of them are skilled players and some always pop a tee shot into the pond. Completely aware that I owe some of them money, I'm sort of hoping that this pond is deep enough that when my brand-new Mizuno soft spike golf shoes hit bottom, my head is not above the waterline.

When I realised that Jimmy, Greg, Assi and George were the next group, frankly, I wanted to squirm like a worm and disappear into the depths of the pond like that famous water monster, the Lock Ness Monster, never to be seen again.

The only significant thought at that moment is that they had not helped my partners bind me to the golf bag and toss me in. Jimmy and Greg might have tossed me in headfirst. I am not looking forward to the next foursome arriving on the 17th tee, but there is no way I can stop them.

I am like an accident victim, strapped in by a seatbelt, waiting to be rescued by the jaws-of-life. Thank God I'm not upside down.

Chapter 2

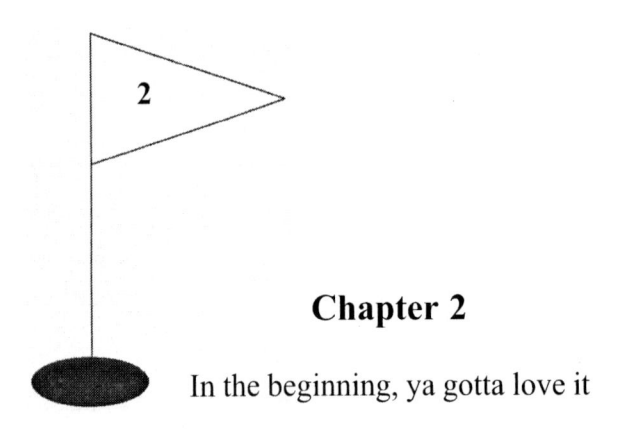

In the beginning, ya gotta love it

Jimmy and Greg, Assi and George aren't the quickest players off the mark, so I have a little time on my hands to review the reason I am, where I am. I love golf. At the age of fourteen I recognized the value of learning to play golf.

My father was a golfer, loved the game, especially on weekends in the summer. When he left the house at five in the morning to get a tee time at the local public course, we could pretty much count on not seeing him again until some time mid afternoon, at which point he'd flop onto the sofa, switch on the television and watch the PGA tour tournament of the week. That would tie him up until about six p.m. on Saturdays and about seven p.m. on Sundays. He was a devoted fan of Arnie, Jack Nicklaus, Johnny Miller, Greg Norman, Freddy Couples, Payne Stewart, and Curtis Strange. When the new crop came out, he liked Ben Crenshaw, Davis Love III, Phil Michelson and then the hyperbole really hit when Tiger Woods stepped into the winner's circle. My mother said my father was more passionate about the game of golf than he was about her. She claimed that she was the classic golf widow. Her husband was not dead, but while he played golf, he left her alone.

In the winter, Dad converted the basement into a driving range. He set up a fishnet and an old mattress against the wall, and put down an emerald green astroturf mat with a rubber tee, and we'd waken on snowy weekend mornings to the swish, whack, thrump of him swinging at and sending a golf ball into the mattress backed net. When Mother had enough of the semi-rhythmic sounds, she'd warn him to stop or she'd toss his precious balls into the snow-covered backyard. At that point he'd switch to putting practice. The whisper soft push of a golf ball toward a putt-returning, electric spring-loaded catcher would end with the thwack of the ball being sent back at him.

His dream was that I would become a pro golfer and one day proclaim that 'my dad taught me the game of golf.'

And you know, watching those PGA professionals play on manicured greens, in warm weather, in places like Arizona, California, Hawaii, Florida, Texas, what Canadian boy with ice in his veins wouldn't want to live and work in tropical weather twelve months of the year? It sure beat shovelling snow.

Dad said if I was good enough, I could get a golf scholarship to an American university and that, considering his limited finances, might be the only way I could get a college education. Education, smed-ucation. I just wanted to live in warmer climates.

So when he signed me up for the junior golf program at Glen Abbey in Oakville I thought, hey, why not? What else am I doing at the age of twelve?

The bonus was that it also got me out of the house and I didn't have to listen to my younger sisters play dolls, tie toys to the cat's tail, dress up the dog in doll's clothes or help Mom clip coupons for that week's groceries. We weren't all that broke, but Mom said Dad spent more on golfing in one weekend than she spent on groceries and somehow she had to save money for a college education for all three of her kids. To be honest, I think she just liked the game; clip the coupon, and save.

I learned a lot in the junior program. First of all came the rules and behaviour of golfers. Dad had taught me the basic swing plane, putting techniques and early betting patterns. In the winter, he'd challenge me to putting contests in the basement for my weekly allowance. I had to learn how to putt or I'd never have enough money to buy smokes. Besides, I had to pay a ten percent premium to my cigarette supplier for taking the risk of buying the addictive drug for a minor.

As the sun was a red ball rising in the east, casting long shadows across the dew covered emerald fairways, as the greens-keeping mowers clipped the top edge of the grass on putting surfaces, as the Ontario sky promised a day outdoors, Dad would drop me off at the golf course. Every day as Dad dropped me off at Glen Abbey golf club I could hear his audible sigh. Every day he'd say, "Wish I'd done this when I was a kid."

At the junior golf program, along with some other kids who didn't know as much about the game as I did, I suffered through the basic technique lessons, the swing plane, the set up, the alignment, the grip, the weight shift, the drive, the fairway shot, the pitch, the putt and all the rules and regulations. We learned the Vardon grip, the semi-overlap grip, the sand shot, the full wedge shot. We spent hours on the driving range, the practice holes and the putting green. And in the beginning I was thrilled to be standing on the practice range, hitting balls like Jack Nicklaus, Freddy Couples, and Davis Love III. Maybe I didn't hit the ball the same, but I was standing in the same place those guys did. We juniors played the course, the same course our heroes walked on. We lugged around our golf bags with dreams of PGA tournament prize money in our pockets.

During my summers at the junior golf program, we were honoured to have some special instructors show us some trick shots. By that time I was so practised out that I needed something to keep me interested and making trick shots became more fun than hitting a hundred yellow balls with my driver. I wanted to know how to make a slice on command, a hook, a lob shot, a pitch and run. I wanted and I needed a challenge. I vividly remember watching Moe Norman on a putting green, thirty feet from the cup, chatting about putting grip, stroke, force, follow through and making three dozen consecutive putts into the hole without so much as a smile on his craggy old face.

I remember watching another hotshot instructor tee it up on the driving range and, on request, hit a high slice, a low fade, a high hook, and a low draw. He talked about the physics and dynamics and the swing plane, and the minor grip change or change to the left foot to manufacture a slice. I found all this very cool stuff to know and I started spending more time practising my trick shots than hitting a ball straight.

Another visiting instructor took us out on the course and showed us how to hit shots from behind trees, around trees, up and over trees, how to make an impossible shot using a right handed club turned upside down and gripped like a leftie. He talked about strategy and making choices with the highest percentage of success.

'Sandy' McIntyre came out one day and taught us how to make bunker shots from fairway bunkers, greenside bunkers, long shots, short flop shots out of steep bunkers, blasting shots and strategic choices. After watching him execute sand shots, we weren't surprised by the accuracy of his nickname.

A former coach from the NCAA, now a college scout, came and taught us about tournament and match play and then watched us play. Supposedly he made notes about us and, in future years, would watch for our successes. He gave us examples of golf resumés that we needed to produce to apply for scholarships at US colleges.

All good lessons.

The golf instructor of the day would give us an hour's worth of lessons and then we'd get out on the course and play as many holes as we could until the sun went down. Marathon golf!

Ah! Those were the days when all we had to worry about was hitting that little white ball as far as we wanted and scoring with as few strokes as possible.

Junior golf was a great time. Except for the back shop duty.

Each of us had to work at cleaning clubs or earn some cash by caddying for paying players. If we weren't caddying, during outside tournaments we'd stand out near the rough and work as spotters for errant shots, quickly finding the ball so their amateur pace of play didn't bog down the whole course. That's when I learned how a lost ball could be truly beneficial.

This rich guy hit his tee-shot into the long rough on fourteen and then hit a provisional off the same tee; I had an eye on the spot where his first ball went into the rough. When he arrived and I told him I knew where his ball was, he told me to go and stand on it, bury it.

I said he could play it.

He slipped me ten bucks if I kept my mouth shut and I thought, why not?

Well, I kept my foot on that ball in the rough, watched him hit his provisional to the green and then make one putt. Bogey golf. I caught up with him later and asked why he didn't play the ball in the rough.

"Odds are I wouldn't get it out of that rough and on the green in one. My provisional was a good shot, so I nailed that one. So it cost me three off the tee, two more to get on and into the hole. Bogey five, instead of a double-bogey six. Odds were with me, kid." Then, with a huge grin on his face, he said he had won the game, gave me a bigger tip and told me I could keep the ball.

"But aren't you supposed to play the ball if you find it?" I asked with stupid innocence.

"Sometimes, kid, stuff that is once hidden is better if it stays that way."

I was an honest kid, but I wanted to see if his philosophy about that shot was correct. I went out to the fourteenth hole, dropped a dozen balls into that rough, and tried to hit the shot to the green. Couldn't be done. It simply couldn't be done. So the old guy was right and he played his provisional and made bogey instead of double bogey. Hmm.

I learned a lot at those junior golf camps. It was a great time.

But at this moment in time, pond water lapped at my chest and my feet haven't touched the bottom of the pond yet. It's as if I'm floating in time; I hope I might just get lucky enough to drift to the bulrushes and have someone pull me out, like the baby Moses.

I glanced up at the 17th tee and my heart turned cold. Situated up there on the tee, the next foursome of Saturday morning players have stalled. I can recognize Jimmy's long, lean figure and bow-legged stance. He looked like a cowboy standing in the morning sun on a western cliff. Greg, who wears his hat like Jesper Parnevik, you know, with the brim turned up like a duck's beak, appeared beside him. And then Assi, a short round character, joined them and finally George Pickering, who used his putter like a cane more often than he used it as a putter. I've taken money off all these guys.

As the four men eye the hole, contemplate the distance, recall their best shots to the green, toss grass into the air to test the wind and consider the best club to use, it reminds me of four Pinkerton agents contemplating their weapon of choice as they looked down on Butch Cassidy and The Sundance Kid right after those two bank robbers jumped off that cliff. I just wish Sundance were in the pond with me, but then I remembered: The Sundance Kid, played by Robert Redford, said he couldn't swim.

For a flashing moment, I consider yelling at them to come and haul me out of the pond, but then I think they probably wouldn't do me the favour. I have taken a lot of money off them in the past. Since they are all good golfers, I have an idea that if I keep my mouth shut, they might just hit their tee shots, walk on down to the green and not even see me. I prayed for that, but what are the odds?

As Jimmy walked down the path from the cliff side tee, his bow-legged gate unmistakable, he yelled at me from the tee side of the pond. "Mikey? What are you doing in the pond?"

"Diving for golf balls. Lost my favourite ball," I said.

"I always thought you were cheap." With his hand in the shape of a loaded and cocked weapon, Greg pointed at me. Smoke drifted up from the cigarette lodged between his fingers. "You still owe me eighty bucks from last weekend's skins game. You got that money on you now?"

"Ah. No. Not today. I'll catch you later."

"Then it ain't worth it to haul you out of there." Greg tossed his cigarette into the pond. The lit cigarette landed close enough to me that I heard it sizzle as it hit the water and polluted my pond. They walked a little faster and disappeared from my view.

I took a deep breath and as silence fell over the air around me, I stared at that piece of pollution. Tiny ripples circle around the cigarette butt disturbing the surface of the pond. Two thoughts come to mind. Will the current in the pond float that soggy cigarette in my direction to crash against my face, and why the hell haven't my feet touched bottom yet?

Chapter 3

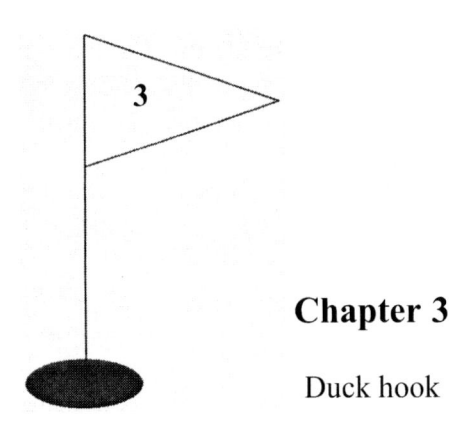

Duck hook

It seems that I'm no longer sinking in the pond on the 17th hole at CrossCreek Golf and Country Club. Water had soaked into my socks a long time ago, my pants are wet, my shirt saturated and the lily pads never looked so beautiful as they did at eye level. Did I mention my golf bag, now strapped to my back, is also still attached to the metal pull cart? I can wiggle my feet, my toes desperately search for the bottom, but I soon decide that the wheels of the cart must have hit bottom, leaving my face above water. Or maybe I am floating a bit because of the hot air I'm gasping to maintain in my lungs.

For the moment, the cliff top 17th tee is empty, but I know that the Saturday tee time roster is loaded and any minute now another foursome will appear on the tee and plan their attack on the green. I eye the lily pads with the pink, white and rose coloured flowers and wonder if the lily pads float free or if they are grounded in the bottom of the pond. I hope the raft of water lilies will float toward me and maybe I can hide behind them until I come up with a way to get out of this pond.

When I manage to drag my water soaked body out of the pond, I'll sneak into the bushes until the Saturday morning golfers have passed, then I'll probably wait until dark and traipse to my car, and drive home to face the rest of my life. If I manage to live so long.

I remember another time that I dragged my waterlogged body home, dripping a trail across campus and hoping I could sneak into the dorm without being caught.

In my second year at North Carolina State, on a half scholarship, studying business accounting and having successfully qualified for the golf team, I, along with some teammates, had been out celebrating a second place finish in the first tournament of the year. It seems to me that was an autumn day, much warmer than you'll find in October in southern Ontario but still there was a chill in the air, and too much beer in the system.

One of us, I forget who, came up with a plan to tease some of the coeds out of the safety of their dorm rooms. Franky Stark, Billy Palmer, Steve Horner and I decided to cause a diversion in the fountain out front of Jefferson dorm. While that noise drew coeds to the front of the building, two of us would go in the back way, run through the halls looking for unoccupied rooms, and steal as many pairs of panties as we could. Then we'd entice the girls to come out and retrieve their panties.

All went according to plan, with Franky and I bouncing around in the fountain, dancing, yelling, singing some repetitive nonsensical phrases, while Steve and Billy ran through the dorm. Half a dozen coeds came out to investigate the noise, and then Steve and Billy arrived with the underpants, which we tossed around and wore like trophies.

One of us heard the sirens and warned the others. We took off, running and dripping, hoping to be safely under covers in our own beds by the time the campus cops tracked us down.

I ran like a drunken banshee, dripped a trail, and crawled in the back window of the guys' dorm building. I raced up the stairs and still soaking wet, crawled into bed, pulled the covers over me and tried to catch my breath, pretend to be asleep and ignore the wet socks, underwear, shirt and jeans that I was still wearing. I'm lucky I wasn't caught.

Billy was, and he was suspended from the team for a month.

Steve, Franky and I commiserated over the punishment but vowed that we couldn't share in Billy's punishment. None of us could afford to be tossed off the golf team and lose our scholarships.

Steve confessed that even if he were caught, there was no way the dean would toss him off the team. He was a 'special case.' I asked him to explain that and he told me that he was a semi-scholarship recipient, but he had also obtained a free loan. His parents claimed they disowned him, he declared bankruptcy and was allowed in as a hardship case. He giggled as he outlined the effectiveness of cheating on his financial report. Steve also happened to be one of our better golfers, but like me was more interested in learning the tricks of the game than playing down the middle.

We saw no challenge in playing down a wide-open fairway. So while other team members perfected their straight long shots, we worked on slices, hooks and trick shots on demand. We were like pool players completely addicted to the game for the challenge of the stymied shot, the carom shots.

In inclement weather we practiced chip shots indoors, lobbing our golf balls into trashcans, short iron shots at targets that we chalked on the gymnastics' team's mattresses. Target golf to a small target was more fun than slamming a drive down the middle of a forty-yard wide fairway.

In the third year, Franky's father started making bets on our tournament standings and Franky told us that his old man made more money if we came in third rather than second, and his father would share some of the winnings. We all needed money for beer and pizzas. Being a numbers wizard, I told the guys what scores we needed to accomplish that task.

I'm not even sure how I became a numbers wizard. I blame my mother and her coupon clipping, shopping arithmetic and compound interest calculations. As a kid, I helped her clip coupons and add up the savings. We subtracted father's golf greens fees, add back in his winnings and decide if we were eating mac and cheese for the rest of the week or would have meat with our dinners.

So when I graduated with a BA in business administration and a fifteenth place finish in the state golf statistics, I knew I wasn't really cut out to be a pro golfer, but I had my degree. Besides, the odds were I'd never make much money on the pro tour. Pop was making a bunch of money on his Saturday morning golf games. That was something I could do, easily. I could win amateur tournaments and take home prizes, and cash from the side bets.

Someday, I would even figure out how Steve managed to declare bankruptcy and cheat on his financial reports but have enough money to own and drive a Porsche.

Just as I figure out my sneaky path from the pond on the 17th hole to my car, so I can slide off the course and quietly go home, the next group of Saturday golfers arrived on the tee. I really want to hide behind some water lilies.

Mark Warner is in that foursome. I can tell it's him by the way he hitches up his plaid pants as he surveys the shot he has to make over my head and to the green. I heard a rumour last week that he is really mad at me for fudging a scorecard and making him pay.

Normally, after a Saturday round of golf, after our 'match cards' beer drinking sessions, we destroy the cards, but someone forgot to rip up the cards and Mark, being the cheap scrounger that he is, pulled them out of the trash and took them home. I knew Mark was really out to fix up the score. If he sees me in the pond, he might just hold my head underwater.

I tried to turn around, hide my face, duck into the water, hold my breath and wait until that foursome passes by. But my feet have not hit bottom and all I can do is wiggle and that creates an underwater surge that causes ripples on the surface. Now, I'm afraid the ripples will draw too much attention to my location. But then, I'm saved as a ball splash-lands at least a dozen yards to my left. I pray to the god of water ponds that I can remain hidden.

"Hey! Is that Mikey?" Brian DeWitt yelled from the cart path as he drove his cart down the hill. The other two players of the foursome were walking and slowly made their way down the hill.

"Where?" someone yelled.

I duck my face under the water so only the back of my head might show, held my breath and counted, hoping and wishing and praying that I can stay down until they pass. But I can hear them.

"There! In the pond."

"I guess that explains why there are only three golfers in the group ahead of those guys."

"How would you know? We're so far behind them; we'll get tagged with slow play. Come on!"

"I'm sure it was Mikey Blaine."

"So what? Who cares? Come on. Hurry up."

"Mikey Blaine owes me money. When I see him, I'm going to nail him for it."

"Yeah? You and everyone else. Get in line!"

I couldn't hear how that conversation finished so I came up for air. I didn't see them, didn't hear them and gasped for air as my chin touched the surface. The pond surface is up to the collar of my black Nike golf shirt. I'm sinking so slowly that, at this rate, I'll have to duck my face in the scummy water every ten minutes to avoid being seen by the rest of the Saturday morning golfers.

If this had been Florida, I'd be worried about surviving in an alligator infested creek without a paddle. But this is southern Ontario on a brilliant autumn day and I plan to be out of the pond before the first snowfall and the pond freezes over.

I start squirming, trying to loosen the straps around my upper body and the bungee cords around my ankles that hold all the golf balls and sand bags in my pants, so I can be free of this mess before the next foursome surveys the hole from the 17th tee.

Unfortunately, all my squirming just causes me to sink a little more.

Chapter 4

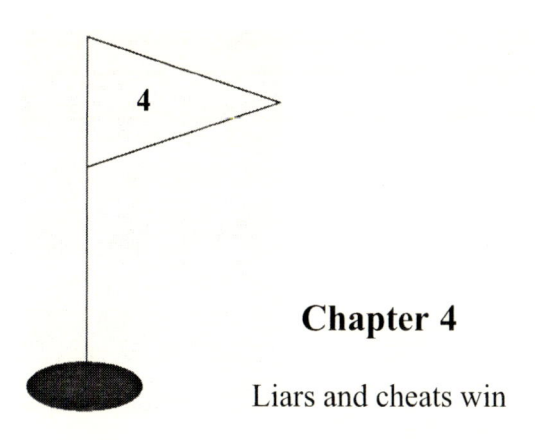

Liars and cheats win

I stopped squirming. And started counting my blessings. The water caresses my throat just above my Adam's apple and the temperature is a balmy seventy-two degrees, which is about eighteen degrees Celsius for us Canadians. In early October we could have had a snowfall by now and I'd be freezing more than just a pocket full of golf balls.

Because I'm so good with numbers, I start to wonder just how many golf balls the guys have stuffed in my bag. I ponder how many of their used Titleist, Staff, Nike, and MAXFLI balls I'll walk away with. I recall that as we stood on the first tee, Jimmy accidentally dropped a golf ball into my golf bag. I didn't pay a whole lot of attention at the time and didn't want to dump my clubs out to get the ball, because then they'd know I carted around fifteen clubs when the regulations clearly stipulate that each golfer may have only fourteen clubs.

It seems to me that Ken offered me a golf ball too. That was on the second tee and because I was about to tee off, I didn't examine the offer.

"I'll just put it in your bag, Mikey."

"I've got some for you, too." Dan offered a handful of old golf balls.

"Sure, I donate them to the junior program," I said as I took a practice swing. Since I'm confessing, I might as well say that was a lie. I use their rejected golf balls for my basement chipping and putting target practice. I only donate the balls to the junior program after I'm finished with them.

I also remember that as I dragged my cart up an incline to the fifth tee, I was amazed at how heavy my bag felt. It never occurred to me that they were planning to anchor me to the bottom of the pond with my own loaded bag. I suppose that out on the golf course, cement shoes are too hard to arrange so they used the next best thing.

But as I count my blessings, I decide that when I get out of this predicament I'll never have to buy another golf ball in my entire life.

Always the optimist, I know I'll get out of this situation. The guys wouldn't let me drown. I've been in some tricky situations and faced larger problems and managed to finagle my way out of those pretty well unscathed.

For instance, as a fresh faced kid just out of college, I landed a decent job in the accounting department of a manufacturing company and knew that my boss was on the path to retirement. While I looked over some old files and annual reports, just to get a feel for the history of the company, I noticed some discrepancies in the numbers and un-recouped employee loans. When I approached my boss about the mismatched numbers, he turned white: paler than a body in a ghost-haunted crypt.

He told me not to worry about the item and he'd look after the uncollected loans. I knew something was pretty fishy and in my spare time did a little more research. When I dug out the old loan agreements, I discovered that the three top executives of the company were the beneficiaries, and he was one of them.

For months I contemplated what to do about the ill-gotten gains. The executives had interest-free money, the company reported a loss and, in essence, the manipulation of the numbers was akin to embezzlement. And on top of that, the three hundred lower level employees, such as myself, who were supposed to get a bonus based on profit, were also victims of this little fraudulent act. No profits equalled no bonus. Again, I thought I did the right thing when I cautiously outlined the repercussions of the mishandled accounting.

He suggested that I not take it personally, but then I explained that I was out about three thousand dollars in bonus payments, and therefore, it was personal.

Next thing I knew, I had a cheque for seven thousand dollars. I was delighted that the bonus payment came through and bought an engagement ring for my girlfriend. By the time I realised my bonus payment was 'hush' money, it was too late to take back the ring from my bride-to-be, get my money back from the jewellery store and return the funds to the company executives who were, in effect, bribing me to keep my mouth shut. Besides, there was no way my bride-to-be would give back the ring.

I had to let the situation play out. The president got a raise, the VP of sales landed a nice bonus, and my boss deposited a larger monthly salary. A couple of years went by and because no one is supposed to talk about salaries, it never occurred to me that the other employees were not getting their bonus payments. I was paid, and I was grateful.

So was my wife.

I left that company and landed a better job with a bigger salary and had more fun at work. Then I read that my old boss and his boss were nabbed for embezzling funds. Because it was a white-collar crime, they both went to the Beaver Creek prison facility in Muskoka, which I heard is like being in jail at the Royal York Hotel. Two years less a day was their sentence and get this: they didn't have to pay back the money because they both declared bankruptcy. Their families went on welfare, so not only did the provincial taxes support the crooks while in jail, their families continued to live on the benefits of the social services system. I knew for a fact that my boss' wife and kids lived in a better house than my wife and I did.

I kept my mouth shut. What if the cops thought I had gone along with the fraudulent manipulation of funds and hauled my ass out of my new job?

The lesson did me well in my quest to make money on the golf course. I had a better-ball partner who frequently lied about his score. Once in awhile our opponents would catch him in the lie and have to recount his strokes. But more times than not, we got away with the miscalculation and would go home with cash in our pockets.

With that thought in mind, I wonder if the cash in my wallet will stay dry. I smile at the image of the fifty-dollar bills floating around in the dryer at home. Truly, the term laundered money would be appropriate.

"Hey, Mikey!" Dick Morrow called to me from the drop area on the tee side of the pond.

My face is in a direct line between where he dropped his ball and the green. I haven't even noticed that a new group has arrived on the tee and that a ball has landed in the water lilies.

"You gonna duck or what?" Dick yelled as he tried a practice swing.

"Betcha get it on the green, Dick," I yelled back at him. "Five bucks says you miss me."

Dick Morrow grinned. "That's tempting but then I'll have to haul you out of there to collect."

"Speaking of hauling me out of here…"

Dick took a mighty swing and the ball skittered across the pond and into the bulrushes over my left shoulder. It was so close I felt the air rush past my ear. Ripples like tidal waves coursed out from the panic beating in my chest.

"Ah, shit. I'm just picking up. Give me a double bogey," he yelled to his partners as he walked around the pond.

Chapter 5

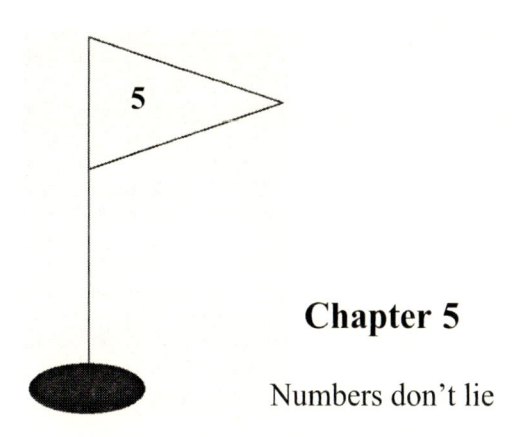

Numbers don't lie

Ripples of water pounding out from my thumping chest smoothed and rolled lazily across the pond. The pink and rose-red water lilies rocked like miniature rowboats on a summer lake. The pounding in my ears, which I'm pretty sure came from the adrenaline burst of fear in my heart, nearly blocked out the whoop of joy as one of the players with Dick sank a putt on the 17th green. I'm not surprised and would lay odds that Rick Kirkwood made the birdie.

Rick is a good player. Five or six handicap. He didn't see me in the pond because typically after he hits his shot from the elevated tee, he picks up his bag and walks down the hill over by the ladies tee and behind the sixteenth green. Bad shots by ladies off that tee or long shots to the sixteenth green can be lost forever in the weed covered hill. None of the ladies try to go into that kind of brush and most of the guys just don't bother, but Rick scavenges for lost balls more than anyone. I'm lucky he didn't see my head and shoulders just above water in the pond of the 17th hole.

Not only is Rick a good player; he's accurate with his tee shots, long irons, chip shots and pitches. Except, he doesn't play well if money is on the line. And if he plays with me, he always thinks he can win. If he had seen me in the pond, I'd probably have a MAXFLI 100 compression golf ball embedded in my forehead. Rick caught me fudging numbers once, and he won't bet with me any more.

Fudging numbers isn't that hard. The numbers need to look right.

First of all, you have to be the one writing down the score, you have to be the one in charge of the numbers. Golfers know that on a five hundred and eight yard par five, like the 18th at Glen Abbey, and you hit driver, three wood, wedge and two putt, you're going to have a five, not a four.

Golfers can picture and remember the shots you made. There are golfers out there, probably right now, sitting in the bar telling tales about every shot they took, on every course they ever played. Reliving every moment of their sub-handicap round.

It's one of the lessons in golf. Imagine the shot, see the shot, feel the shot, execute it, then vividly remember it out loud and bore the hell out of every non-golfer within earshot. Golfers have memories and it seems to improve if they can picture the hole. They'll remember the way you played the hole, where the drive landed, where the next shot went, the enormously long putt you made, or didn't make. Now here's the thing, if you're the scorer and you've fudged the numbers, don't retell the game in too much detail.

My wife is still pretty confused about how I can relive every shot of a five hour round of golf but can't remember to pick up milk on the way home. I told her it's a picture perfect memory. Then, following my advice, if she wants me to remember to bring home something from the grocery store, she tapes pictures of what I'm supposed to remember to the dashboard of my car. I have to peel them off before I get out of the car at the golf club.

As the official scorer you're supposed to calculate accurately. But if you want to fudge numbers on the scorecard, you have to be very good with numbers. I mean good, like an accountant is good with numbers. Accountants know how things add up, how good or how bad a balance sheet can appear. Tax accountants know how to fudge tax filings, so you pay less taxes. They wouldn't call it fudging the numbers, but they'd call it 'using the rules.' The rules, they say, are there for your benefit. The rules are applied equally to all, just like the rules of golf.

Rick Kirkwood knows the rules of golf. He knows how to use them to his benefit. Rick is also an accountant and, a little known detail, he works for Revenue Canada. That is something he doesn't want just anyone at the club to know. For a good reason. If the guys knew he might be the one who audited their taxes, he would be headfirst in the pond.

Just as he is precise and methodical in his work, he is methodical in his golf swing pre-shot routine. There he'll be, standing at his ball, middle of the fairway, eyeing the green like a sniper eyeing the latest goof-off politician. Rick will look at the distance marker on the sprinkler head, glare at the flag, and judge the exact distance to the hole. He'll pull out an iron, take a practice swing from behind the ball, then beside the ball, eye the target, set his feet, touch his thigh, re-grip, re-grip, eye the hole and finally hit the damn ball. He has to be one of the slowest players at the club. We're lucky he's a good player. If he were a bad player and we had to suffer through that routine for every shot in his one hundred-plus round, we'd be on the course for seven hours instead of the usual four and a quarter.

Players at ninety percent of the courses in our area take five hours or more to play a round of golf. Speed of play is one of the best things about playing at CrossCreek. Speed wins and winning money from Rick Kirkwood at match play golf has an added touch of irony. In my small way, I am ripping off an agent of Revenue Canada.

One time, when I laughed about that happy fact, Rick told me I should declare my winnings as income.

Yeah, right.

Just like my boss declared the income he got from exaggerating on his expenses. Just like drug dealers declare their profits, just like those phoney fund-raisers send the money to the charities for which they are supposedly raising money. And just like politicians who take their staff out for expensive dinners on taxpayers' money and have no regrets, I never regret my winnings.

With happy memories of taking money off Rick, I looked up at the 17th tee to see who might lead my rescue team. I sincerely hope the odds are in my favour, but I had a lot of calculating to do. I had to believe that the best man to manage my rescue would be the man I had lost to more often than not.

As I watched the man on the tee swing and then yank on his follow through, and watch the ball on the trajectory of a duck hook to his left, my right, over the end of the pond, I knew it was Freddy Gordon. And since Freddy liked to play with Ed Kelly, Don Franklin and Danny Compton, I had this foursome narrowed down. Then I analysed their capabilities and figured I'll only have to bury my face in the pond once. The problem is, from this distance I can't tell who is who. I know for a statistical fact that I've never had to pay off bets to any of these guys. Odds are not in my favour of this foursome rescuing me. My best bet is to stay as well hidden as possible.

I ducked my face into the pond for all three of the rest of the foursome and raised my face just enough to watch for them to walk down the cart path. Ed, Don and Danny headed to my left and I'll be hidden by the bulrushes and water lilies at that end of the pond. But Freddy walked right toward me then along the edge of the pond to my right. He's scavenging for golf balls along the tee side of the pond. If I stay very still he won't see me, but I'm getting chilled and the swamp water smell is making my nose itch. I started doing all the physiological things I can to prevent the sneeze. Stopping a sneeze without using your hands isn't all that easy.

Then, Freddy scooped a ball from the edge of the pond, looked at it, scowled and tossed the ball like a lob shot, right into the middle of the pond. Water splashed my face. He missed me by about four inches. I sneezed and then cleared my sight by blinking; Freddy was reaching for another ball but frozen in time and staring right at me.

"Mikey?"

"Hi, Freddy. I see you hit your usual duck hook."

"What the hell are you doing in there?" he whispered. Then he squatted lower.

I looked to the left. The other three players have disappeared from my sight line. I whispered, "Paying off a bet? Can you help me out of here, Freddy?"

"Are you stuck?"

"Yeah, you could say that."

"Why don't you just swim out?"

"Ah. I'm tied to my golf bag."

"The one with fifteen clubs?" Freddy stood up.

"I don't have fifteen clubs in my bag," I lied.

He knew it.

"Tell you what." He adjusted his bag. "You admit to having fifteen illegal clubs in your bag and I'll try to figure a way to get you out."

"Freddy, I don't have fifteen illegal clubs. But I can tell you, there has to be a few dozen balls in my bag, dropped in by my fellow players, just to weigh me down."

"I guess, for a sandbagger, that's like wearing cement shoes." Freddy laughed and walked away. "Hey, guys!"

"Freddy, don't tell anyone," I whispered.

He didn't say anything more, that I heard. I watched him hit a lob shot to the green and I'd lay odds that he two-putted for a bogie. I stared at where Freddy had last been until there were four of them standing there.

I smiled.

Well, in reality, I winced.

"You want me to tell your wife, you're in there, Mikey? Tell her that you'll be late getting home?"

"No, don't tell anyone. Just get me out."

"Maybe after we finish. I've got a really good game going. May celebrate with a couple of beers. Hang in there, Mikey." Freddy waved.

They just laughed and walked to the eighteenth tee. Considering my success in convincing the guys to form a rescue team, I had better odds organising pallbearers for my funeral.

My groan rolled across the smooth-as-glass surface. I sure as hell don't want them calling my wife and telling her I'm stuck in the middle of the pond. The way things have been going lately, she'd dig me out after the last snowfall in southern Ontario. Or, as she would put it, "when hell freezes over."

Besides, I don't have 15 illegal clubs. I have 15 clubs, but that is only one over the legal limit.

Chapter 6

The year of living idly

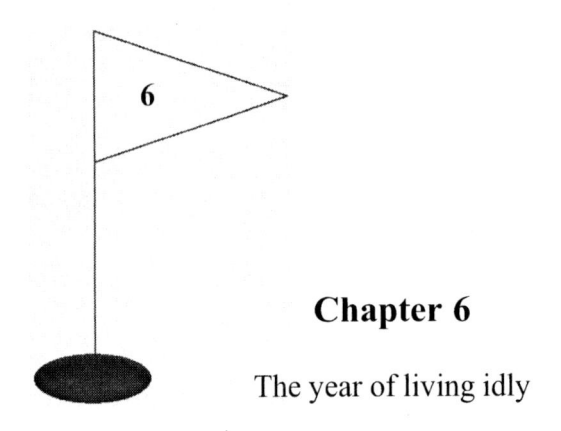

This day is passing about as quickly as my year of total unemployment. If the saying, 'Time flies when you're having fun,' is true, then, for a fact, the opposite is equally true. It's been a year in which I've had very little fun. It's also the year that Dad took an unplanned trip to the heavenly golf course in the sky, where he, hopefully, is enjoying his time.

I wish I'd placed Dad's favourite 'bull's eye' putter and a dozen golf balls in his casket before the golf gods took him to that dream golf course in the sky. In his last days, as he lay in bed at home trying to recover from the latest round of chemo therapy, he and I relived, in descriptive detail, our favourite golf holes, memorable golf shots, the colour of the morning sun that day I won the Ontario Amateur tournament. We talked about the ideal golf course, the understated talent of Mike Weir. Dad would have been so proud of a Canadian winning the Masters Tournament.

He reminded me that I was the same size as Mike and had just as much potential. But Dad never knew about Mike's win and I knew I'd never live up to Mike Weir's potential. I was Michael Blaine, not Mike Weir, and I am stuck in a swamp, waiting for a soggy extinction, deliriously looking forward to the tee times that Dad and I will have on the heavenly golf course in the sky.

With silence and time on my hands, I looked around at my floating companions. An idyllic floating lily pad shifted as if an unseen underwater hand guided its course. Water lilies and lily pads lived idly, rest on the surface, and camouflage, with perfect laziness, what lurks beneath.

I began to worry about what lurked beneath the surface of my year of living idly. I like to think that in the long run, my year of living idly paid off. I met my girlfriend that summer and improved my technique.

I had been laid off from my job, downsized, re-engineered, let go. With summer fast approaching, I didn't mind having the time to work on my golf game. My wife, Sharon, wasn't too happy about our lowered income, but I was pretty cock-sure that I'd get another job by the end of the summer, and I prayed nightly to the golf god that I wouldn't get a job before the first frost closed the golf course.

Melanie is a teacher, so we both had the summer off. At the beginning of the summer, I didn't plan to find a girlfriend. I was married, so nailing another woman wasn't on my agenda.

My agenda simply involved learning how to be a better golfer. At that point, I was an eighteen handicapper, and being one who likes to see good numbers, I wanted, worked for, and dream of a lower handicap. A single digit handicap would be solid evidence that I am a good golfer.

However, being laid off and eligible for employment insurance, I had to attend the 'how to get a job' workshops. And in the beginning of my benefit period I attended all the information seminars I could find. That was in January, and in Ontario, I sure wasn't going to be out on the snow-covered fairways. I attended the sessions and took all the information to heart. I wrote and re-wrote my resumé, sent out specific cover letters, adjusted my resumé for the job description, talked to recruiters, read the careers section of all the local papers. I researched companies on the web, took all the mind-bending career and psychological assessment tests. I studied the highly effective habits of successful executives, books like *What They Don't Teach You at MBA Business Schools; Going for the Gold, Getting the Prize; The Peter Principle*. All valuable stuff. As I practised my putting on the emerald green astroturf in the basement, I even rehearsed my interview techniques.

Like a miss-hit golf shot, the economy had dropped into a swampy pond. Dot-coms were selling off their equipment, laying off staff. Auto dealers weren't selling vehicles, auto plants were threatening layoffs in Oakville, which was probably because the head office in Detroit hadn't worked out their Alabama plant labour contract and used Oakville's announcement as an intimidating threat to the International Brotherhood of the UAW. One of my golfing buddies who knew someone who worked at the local auto plant alleged that the USA's head honcho had not warned the Oakville boss that the announcement was being leaked to the press.

I felt a little sorry for the head guy in Oakville who, even though he was the most senior executive in Canada, had not been forewarned about the impending doom and gloom news.

At any rate, that caused auto parts manufacturers to lay off production workers who, in turn, had no money to spend on anything, which, in turn, slowed the economy even more. Then, Lady Luck, as if scorned, dished out the hype about SARs, a severe acute respiratory virus, and took a revenge-filled swing at the economy. Companies were locking their doors because they didn't want any infections walking in the door. Well, I wasn't invited to walk in any doors either.

On the upside, I remembered in a previous job, being one of the staff members who was not laid off, I remained, doing the work of those who had been let go, and scared silly that I'd be next on the 'lay off' list, working unpaid overtime just to keep up, listening to the escalating fears of those of us waiting for the dismissal slip. Back then, I decided that if I ever had a choice, I'd rather be laid off than left behind.

That year of living idly, I was very picky about the companies I applied to. Hating gridlock, I wanted someplace close to home. I wanted to be in an interesting industry, with growth potential and a decent salary. And since the economy wasn't co-operating in my job search, my prayers for not finding a job until the end of golf season could easily come true.

"It's a matter of luck," I told my wife. "Timing and luck." I switched the channel from the women's golf to the PGA pre-game show for the Masters' championship coverage from Augusta, Georgia. They were making all kinds of predictions about who would win. As a true blue Canadian golfer, I had a bet on Mike Weir, Canada's answer to how to succeed at golf. Mike was my inspiration.

So far Mike had had a good year, winning two tournaments. Sure, Tiger could outdrive Mike, but Mike's drives are more accurate and his short game is phenomenal. He's from southern Ontario. He's a Canadian, and even if he lives in Utah, he still represents Canada on the PGA and world tours. And he is solidly working on his short game, in his basement. We have a lot in common.

His win at the Masters was motivational. As I watched the last round in my living room, as he assessed every ten-foot putt, my knuckles were white from gripping and re-gripping, squeezing the blood out of the shaft of my Ping putter. He'd stand over the putt and I held my breath until the ball clunked into the hole. I danced and yelped "YES!" just like those face-paint covered football fans we see on televised games. I'm sure every Canadian golfer worth his or her salt was doing the same thing I was. We were holding our collective breaths, clasping hands and praying for Mike Weir to win this green jacket. For Canada!

Ah, the sweet sound of success. Mike won the green jacket and I won a bundle of cash for my pocket. When my wife found out how much I'd won, she asked me if I could make any more money playing golf.

"I'm not a professional."

"Then maybe you should find a job. Or something. Didn't any of those 'how to find a job' seminars help at all?"

"You mean like the seminar where I'm encouraged to share job search ideas with the group that the employment insurance office arranged for me to attend with people in the same situation? Like the one I went to with fourteen other people, twelve of who were gravel truck drivers? Yeah, it was great to share ideas with a bunch of guys who could barely speak English, didn't know how to type let alone understand the concept of a resumé. You mean the seminar with the so-called instructors who didn't understand that gravel truck drivers and financial department managers don't have a lot of common ways to find jobs? Oh, sure, it was sort of amusing to watch the young lady instructor wearing a silk blouse, linen skirt, high heels and diamond earrings tell the truck drivers to put on a suit and polish his shoes. I can just see Guido climbing out of his dump truck wearing his shiny Gucci shoes, Italian silk tie, and an Armani suit for an interview at a rock quarry. Can't you?"

She hesitated, cocked her head to one side and said, "Well, can you drive a dump truck?"

The thump she heard was my forehead banging on the desk.

"Well, didn't they teach you anything at those seminars?" she asked.

I heard her walk away but continued to rock my head. After I lifted my head off the desk and rubbed the self-inflicted goose egg on my forehead, I got to thinking. There are more ways to pocket money than hanging around in an office, waiting for the boss to realise that I knew he was scamming the company or Revenue Canada or both. Waiting for the boss to get caught didn't pay off for me. I had been let go. Not him.

As I watched replay after replay of Tiger holding the green jacket for Mike Weir to pull on, I decided that I'd have to reapply all those suggestions and set my plans in motion. I'd follow the advice I received from all those 'how to find a job' seminars and set attainable goals and document achievements for myself.

"You're right," I told my wife.

"You're going to drive a dump truck?"

"No, but I'm going over all those 'how to find a job' seminar notes. I'm going to set goals."

"That's nice." She smiled and asked me what I wanted for dinner.

I set a goal: to lower my handicap. I broke that into attainable achievements; lower my handicap one stroke at a time. I narrowed down the skills to do that, one skill at a time; sand shots; pitch shots; putts; know the rules; trick shots; lob shots. I then split the goals into the specific skills that I'd need. I started with the basics; grip; alignment; follow through; and pose.

One morning, my wife caught me, naked, in front of her full-length mirror in the bedroom, posing in my back swing and follow-through positions.

She giggled and asked, "Are you supposed to point that, like that?"

She wasn't pointing at my toe.

Her giggling and pointing distracted me from my goal. As a compromise, I tried to teach her how to swing a club, but as I watched her uncoordinated jerky movements and watched her wave the club at my naked athletic form, I feared for the loss of my personal equipment.

Sharon started asking about the world of golf. To that point, her education into the workings and wonders of golf had all been from watching golf on television, which she admitted she watched only because I safeguarded the remote control until I fell asleep. Then she'd rip it from my grip and change the channel. Of course I'd wake up and want the handset back, so then she'd ask me dumb questions like, why is a sand trap called a bunker and why is a sand wedge called a wedge? Who really cares that Davis Love THE THIRD has the best 'sand-save' average?

"Sharon, Mike Weir is about to putt. Quiet please."

"You think he can hear me?" she'd ask. "Wow! Ain't technology wonderful. Talk about interactive television."

"Shush."

About that point, I remembered something my father said, "A man has to have a place to go for just doing man things."

So in my basement training area, I arranged a worktable, a couple of full length mirrors, moved my computer from my upstairs office, set up computer files, and planned to document and track my milestones and achievements. I planned to lower my handicap and increase my odds of winning. I had a goal.

As spring rolled into southern Ontario and rain delayed the opening of the golf courses, other than practising in the basement, my only other option was visits to the driving range. I was just itching to test out my new grip, my new pose, and my new swing. Just like Mike, all winter I practised in the basement and continued to work on my short game more than on my long shots. But I had to get out there on the astroturf tee and see my three hundred yard dead-straight drives, test my theories on how to work the ball into a fade to the right or a draw to the left.

There's a practice facility not far from where I live. It's been rated one of the best in Canada and recently they updated the layout and installed a second level of tee boxes, one floor up from ground level. And both teeing areas are covered. One can practice in the rain without getting wet.

The target areas look like they had painted the ground. It's astroturf. Green for putting surfaces, blue for ponds, yellow for sand. Flags fluttered in the breeze as vehicles hummed along the QEW just beyond the trees. Much to my severe disappointment, my grip failed me, my old swing came back with a vengeance and I had a huge slice that went out about a hundred and twenty yards and then immediately headed right. I needed to work on this game, a lot.

The facility had real sand traps from which to practice bunker shots and real putting greens to chip to, to putt on. It was a surrogate golf course. And with some planning, one could imagine playing a game of golf.

On one of those rainy, windy, blustery days when even practising from a covered tee box was pretty useless, I was sitting in the pro shop snack area with some guys and we came up with a scorecard for a game at the practice facility.

This is how it worked. If my shot landed and stayed on the nearest aimed-for green, it would be a worth one point. The next farthest away was worth two points and the farthest green was worth three points. If my shot landed on the pond, it was a minus two. We worked out a rotation of aiming for the greens and actually made up some scorecards.

Then I made bets with the guys. And I kept track of my winnings. Not bad for an eighteen handicapper, when there were no handicaps allowed. I spent hours trying to figure out how to use handicaps and win more often in a game where handicaps don't count. As the wet spring turned to an overheated spring, I gave up that manipulation of numbers and turned my attention to real golf and real handicaps on real golf courses.

The weather improved and in late April, after Mike Weir's Masters win, we were all out there, playing the course, complaining about how the fairways had no roll because it was too wet, how the winter had ruined the greens and our putting. In general, handicaps went up for everyone, except mine.

I was losing my small wagers and being unemployed I couldn't afford to lose too much. I decided that a low handicap was fine, if all I really wanted to do was brag about how low it was. But if I wanted to earn some cash on the course, I needed a better game plan, a better handicap. In this case, a better handicap doesn't mean lower.

I stayed up nights trying to figure out the calculations and how to get a better handicap. Then, as if to kibosh that plan, I met Melanie near the chipping green.

She is attractive but even more attractive is her ability to pitch her shots toward a hole. I was curious about how she could hit a ball to within a foot of the miniature flagpole, no matter how near or far away the hole happened to be.

She explained her technique. "The safer shot is to get the ball rolling on the green as soon as possible. You want it to roll, not bounce all over the place. Judge the distance from the ball to the green. Find a spot on the green where you want your ball to land, match your back swing to the forward swing, and on the follow through, finish with the top point of your forward swing aimed at the spot where you wanted the ball to land. You judge the distance to roll by knowing what your club will do. A seven iron shot will roll farther than a nine iron pitch shot."

As I watched her, I asked what she taught in high school.

"Geometry," she said with a winning smile.

That made sense. It made a lot of sense.

"It's good to know for reading breaks on a green, too." Then she added, "And shooting pool. It all comes down to knowing the angles. The trajectory, the speed, the lay of the land."

I liked numbers but I never realised that learning geometry in high school would pay off on the golf course. "I suppose you're pretty good with algebra, too?" I asked.

"Algebra is just formulas. And you'll need some algebra to figure out distances. Geometry helps figuring out the distance and how to get from point A to point B. But I'm surprised you asked for a pitching lesson."

"Surprised at what?"

"Guys don't usually ask for directions, so you asking for a pitching lesson..." She hit a pitch shot and the ball rolled into the hole.

"Let me make a pitch," I said, with my best smile and sighed. "Teach me and I'll buy you a drink."

"Make it dinner and you're on."

The expansion of my chest made water ripple and tickle my chin. I looked up from my reverie to see who would be the next foursome on the 17th tee. I couldn't tell who exactly they were and tried to remember the tee time roster. I squinted at the upright bodies on the tee and by his pre-shot routine or his swing, tried to figure out who it was. If I could calculate who was teeing it up first, and identify him, I could surmise who his playing partners were.

Then one of them started biting his nails. Maurice Dodds always bit his nails as he eyed the 17th green. Maurice is a weekend duffer, loves the game, plays like a smuck, never took a lesson in his life and shoots more balls into this pond than any other member of the club. It's almost written history how one afternoon, he came out here after a round of golf, with his set of clubs and a wastebasket size bucket of the balls he scavenged from the fescue.

As the legend goes, he swallowed a few too many beers after losing another five bucks in the Saturday morning game and now was determined to hit at least one ball onto the 17th green or he'd toss his clubs into the pond and quit the game entirely. No one believed he would do it.

That sunny day in July, about a dozen well-watered guys, including me, accompanied him. As Maurice dumped his fifth shot into the pond, I started placing bets. Buck a shot.

The dozen coaches started yelling at Maurice, cheering him on, giving him advice.

"Swing easy, Maury."
"Take a longer iron, Maury."
"Swing harder, Maury."
"You can do it."
"You the man!"

Maurice's hands were bleeding by the time he quit for the day. Not one shot had made it over the pond. Some had been short of the water but most had gone in the pond. Plunked in, skittered in, on the fly, pop up lob shots. The harder he tried, the worse he got.

"How many balls do you figure he put in the pond?" one golfer asked as we trekked back to the club for another beer.

"I lost fifty-seven dollars. A buck a shot."

I kept betting on Maurice to get to the green. He appreciated the support. It was a small price to pay. Over the years, I've taken probably seven or eight hundred off Maurice and more from the others.

"I didn't start betting until he'd dunked about six," I said.

"So there's at least sixty golf balls in the pond."

We heard a splash and looked back. Sure enough, Maurice had thrown his clubs, bag and all, into the pond. Rumour has it that Maurice came back the next morning with a scuba diver who retrieved his golf bag and as many balls as he could find.

As I looked up at Maurice on the tee, I wondered if I'm standing on his collection of un-retrieved golf balls and that prevented me from downing.

Then I realised that in my current situation the odds of not being hit were not in my favour. Maurice had made the green with a well-executed shot from the elevated tee on the 17th hole only twice all summer. And I'm pretty much in the middle of the pond.

"You the man, Maury! You the man!" I yelled.

Four upright bodies on the tee bent forward. One shaded his eyes, one shaded the sides of his face and visor. To me, from that distance they looked like those three monkeys. See no evil, speak no evil, hear no evil. Given that I'm a hundred yards away, I can't hear what they're saying.

"You the man! Maury! You the man!" I yelled again.

I can see Maury's practice swing, which isn't all that good. And I saw the sun glint off the club, so I know he isn't using his driver, which is what he should use on this hole. On a hazard-less hole his drives travel only about a hundred yards and then roll forty yards. There is no way he can get over the pond with an iron. If the pond were frozen his ball might skitter to the green. But Maury likes to think he can hit like the long ball wizards and persists in using an iron.

Fortunately, for me, at the moment the pond is not frozen.

"Maury! It's me! Mikey! Don't hit me, Maury."

The foursome on the tee turned away as if they didn't hear me.

Maury took another practice swing.

"Maury, it's me! Mikey." I bellowed.

He stood up to his ball. I counted his practise swings, always three, and then I took a deep breath and put my face in the water. A ball slamming into the back of my head or my shoulders would hurt, but it wouldn't kill me. I heard the splash and came up for air.

Duncan Bober was on the tee and I have no worries about Duncan. He's a ten handicapper and has no problem ever getting over this pond. I sighed. I waited. I watched.

The foursome came down the hill and stood at the edge of the pond looking at me.

Maury blinked, dropped his ball and then made a nice lob shot over the pond.

"Nice shot, Maury," I said.

"You know what this reminds me of?" Duncan Bober mused. "Reminds me of the carnival at my kid's high school, the one where you toss a hardball at a target and the principal falls into the tub of water."

"You know, Mikey, you'd have a better view of the green if you were at that end of the pond." Daniel Gerard pointed west.

"You don't have a catcher's mitt with you in there? You could catch all the badly hit tee shots." Duncan laughed.

"Mikey, while you're in there, not doing much, see if you can find my seven iron. Remember when I threw my bag into the pond in July? It was the only one we never found. Have a look for me, would you, Mikey?"

"Sure, Maury. I thought you were going to quit golfing?"

"This game? I love this game. I could never give up this game. Not until death do us part."

"His wife likes to have the day to herself. She never sends out a search party," Duncan said.

"Speak for yourself." Maury elbowed Duncan and marched around the pond.

That got me to thinking about my wife. I wondered if she would miss me enough to send out a search party. An air-sea rescue? The way things have been going lately, she might just throw me a bag of cement.

She might be very happy that my life insurance premium payments are up to date, but Sharon won't be happy that Revenue Canada wants to subtract death taxes, now called probate fees. But maybe she could ask Rick for some tax advice. She liked him. But knowing him, he'll ask if I declared my golf winnings. Since my wife doesn't know about all my golf winnings, she wouldn't be too happy to find out I've been spending most of my winnings on my girlfriend.

I can just picture the two of them, my wife and my girlfriend, standing side by side, arms linked, at my funeral. In my mind, one would be dressed in black, the other in red, symbolically cohesive, and before dirt is shovelled on my casket, the mourners would toss used golf balls onto my coffin. The balls would bounce and echo in the gravesite.

My wife would attempt to throw in my extremely valuable Scottsdale, Arizona, Ping putter that I have forgotten to retrieve from the house and my golfing girlfriend would jump in after it. Other mourners would help her out of the pit and they'll probably go back to the golf club to celebrate as if someone had accomplished a hole-in-one, and I was the one in the hole. They'd celebrate more than my life.

I wondered if, as a final symbolic gesture, a mourner at my funeral would toss in a flowering water lily. I'm beginning to believe that just like everyone else, I can't cheat taxes or death. Both are inevitable.

Chapter 7

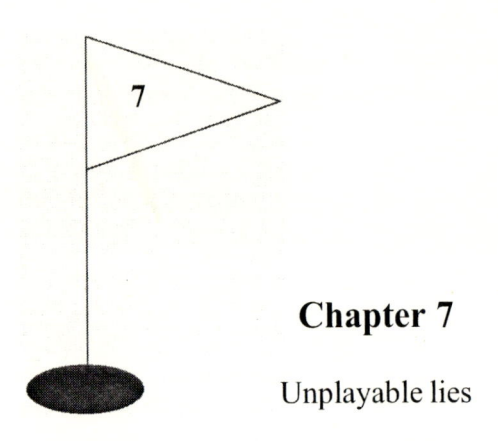

Unplayable lies

Cheating was easier than I thought. I had to plan ahead and work with the best resources available. Working with the rules and managing resources is one route to success. I learned that if I thought there is the tiniest chance that someone, like my wife, might try to find me, I had to work with my pro shop staff. I had to remember that the rules of golf exist and the pro shop staff is there for my benefit.

Normally, when I get to the golf course, the first thing I do is check in with the pro shop. I walk into the pro shop, chat with them about the weather, the course conditions, verify the tee time, make sure they knew my name, and then tell the pro shop staff I'll be on the driving range.

One day a married friend of mine didn't do that. So there he was out on the driving range, happily shooting balls at the target flags, whiling away a couple of hours. When he got home, his wife was livid. She had called the pro shop and asked if they could get a message to her husband. When the pro shop staff told her they had not seen her husband she became furious.

She figured that her husband had been lying about his whereabouts and was probably off schmoozing with some floozy. This man, who had never in his married life been with another woman, had to tip toe around the house for months. So you have to let the pro shop guys provide an alibi.

Okay, so that was me. And I felt like my mother had put a curfew on my fifteen-year-old, grade ten butt. Which happened the same summer I stole Mom's car, borrowed twenty bucks from her wallet, and skipped classes to be with my girlfriend. Come to think of it, Sharon was my girlfriend in high school and she is a lot like my mother.

That summer of learning to live idly, after I showed my face in the pro shop, with a couple of borrowed demo clubs in my hand, I'd wander out to the driving range. Melanie, my girlfriend, would park near the driving range and I'd lay my clubs in the back seat of her car, crawl in, stay low while we cruised on over to her place for a little morning fun. Later on, she'd drop me off near the driving range and I'd finish my range practice. Then she and I would hook up for a game of golf. Since my wife never played golf and never came to the club, I was pretty safe.

As the pond water lapped at my neck, I decided that cheating really is easier than you think. Just remember the rules of the game. The PGA sports tournament commentators are forever claiming the rules are there to make the game fair to everyone and to benefit the player. Just like there are rules in golf, which exist for my benefit, I suppose there are rules in marriage and relationships. If someone wrote enforceable rules for a marriage, laid out like the Royal Canadian Golf Association 'Rules of Golf,' I bet they'll make a small fortune. On the other hand, if I knew those rules could be enforced, would I ever get married?

But I suppose the real key is, that more often than not, all us players go by the honour system. In golf, to speed up play, if a player has hit a ball that might be lost and possibly never found, he declares that he is hitting a provisional shot. Then you look for the first ball and if found, play that ball, but if it is really lost, then play the provisional ball, or go back to the original position before hitting the lost ball. It's a lot faster to play a provisional than walk back up to the tee. And there is a time limit on how long you can look for the ball. Some guys don't even look.

The most obvious place to lose a ball is in the fescue. Fescue is that extra long grass beyond the long grass called rough. The fescue grass in midsummer is high enough to touch your knees and in some places tall enough to hide a Volkswagen. Well-watered fescue has a network of stalks and if you just dropped a ball from your hip, it could burrow down into the undergrowth like a mouse trying to hide and never be seen again. Trying to hit out of that kind of fescue usually just make matters worse.

A couple of years ago, there was a tournament in which Davis Love III was leading, but he yanked a tee shot into outrageously ugly brush. He hit a provisional, then made a passing glance at the ugly brush that no doubt would hide his 'lost ball' and told the search team to stop looking. More than once he told them to stop looking. The ball was lost. By then everyone knew that Tiger had yanked his tee shot into a difficult position, so Davis wasn't out of the winner's circle just yet, if only he could hit his provisional ball onto the green. A difficult but not impossible shot.

But just as Davis was ready to hit his next shot from the really decent provisional ball position, some yahoo spectator found the original ball. Then Davis had to play that 'lost' ball, by going back on the line of flight, dropping the ball in a playable location and hitting from there, with no chance to get to the green. He would have had a better score if that ball could have stayed lost and he could have hit his provisional ball. He would have had a better chance if that spectator had kept his mouth shut. From my position on the sofa, I could see the anger in Davis' eyes.

Occasionally a golfer can find his ball in that ultra long grass. A lot of us self-deceptive macho-types try to slash our way out of the mess and plan to move the ball forward. I've tried this a few times but more often than not I manage to help the ball slide deeper and deeper into the tangled web of fescue stalks. I've tried flashing my way out of arguments with my wife, but the more my mouth volleyed with fibs, the deeper my predicament became. The more I hack at the lies and falsehoods, the deeper the ugly brush I'll be in. If feasible, declare an unplayable lie, take the one stroke penalty and move on.

In golf there are rules about such things as immovable obstructions, like fences, which are placed to protect other golfers from errant shots. The rules of golf allow for a player to move his ball without a penalty so he can continue play. When I arrive at a golf course, I check the scorecard for local rules. This is where I find a description of the immovable objects on this particular course. In most cases I can get a free lift, no penalty. If wives came packaged with scorecards that listed the local attributes of an immovable object, we husbands wouldn't be in such deep fescue so often. We could just spout the rule, take a free lift and move on.

In the honour system of golf, it's best to check with the playing partners about invoking an unplayable lie before moving the ball. It's the honourable thing to do, but it's like asking for permission.

When I was in the middle of my career, I didn't ask my boss for permission to stay late. I stayed until I got the job done. I didn't ask my boss for permission to deny some salesman's expenses. I didn't have to ask my wife for permission to stay late at the office. And since the golf club was where I earned money, I wasn't about to ask my wife for permission to stay later at the club than I initially planned.

Nobody asked my permission before they wrapped golf bag straps around me, pinning my arms to my sides, or when they tied bungie cords around my pant cuffs and dropped bags of sand down my pants, or when they used their own bag straps and tied me to my bag and cart. And I am damn sure nobody asked for my permission before they tossed me feet first into the pond.

Now all I have to do is to figure out how to get out of this predicament.

I didn't see anyone on the 17th tee, which meant the next foursome was playing way too slow and would get a nasty warning letter from the management. When I recalled the tee time list, it seems to me that this group, or the next, had at least one guest in the foursome. Guests tend to play slower, especially if they've never been to our course before.

But it also means I might have time to plan my escape from the pond.

From my low to the ground position I can almost see the greenskeeper's storage sheds and equipment. All the mowers are lined up in a row beside the shed. If I could convince one of the young guys who cut the greens and rake the traps to use a mower to drag me out, I... but this being a Saturday, the staff had cut the greens first thing in the morning and then gone home.

I'll have to come up with another plan.

Up on the cliff top tee the next group appeared. By the shape of them, I know who they are right away. Philip Perry, who has the profile of a large pear, is easy to recognize. They all were distinguishable even from this distance and more obvious because they frequently play together. Jeff Grafton III is a lawyer, about my size, five foot six and one hundred and forty pounds. Manni Spadifori, whose aura precedes him, and that aura sometimes looks like a ghostly bodyguard, carries his driver like a double-barrelled shotgun and is equally as easy to recognise. The fourth player is George Warburton, who grips his club like he's shifting gears on a Harley. He has a long ponytail of black hair that fluttered in the cliff top breeze. George usually arrives at the course on a Harley Davidson that is worth more than my car. Rumours floated around that George used to belong to the Hell's Angels but is now retired. He has never corrected the rumours.

Philip doesn't scare me. Jeff is my size so there was no fear there, but Manni and George have a kind of presence even before they enter a room. I don't know why I even tried to hustle some money out them. I must have been hung over. Or blind drunk.

My thought as I watch them tee off from the cliff is that I had no worries about a ball landing in the pond or on my head. They are all good golfers. If I could stay underwater for oh, ten minutes or so, I'll be safer than if they see me in this position. If the rumours are true, Manni might just order up a pair of cement shoes or pull a Beretta from his bag.

My chest squeezed tighter than when I fell through the ice on the hockey rink that we ten-year-olds fashioned on the Port Credit River too soon in the winter. The almost frozen water yanked the air from my lungs and panic squeezed at my brain.

Obviously, I was pulled out of that mishap, but I was forever afraid to skate on thin ice. I should have recognised that betting with Mannie and George is a lot like that day when I was ten. Now I hope that the soft-spoken biker and the perpetually smiling Mannie would just ignore my plight and walk on by.

The ever-observant Jeff Grafton III, a criminal lawyer who started his career with undergraduate courses in psychology, 'to learn how to examine and understand the jury,' spotted me when he was halfway down the hill. Either that or he was grinning at his ball on the green. I'd seen the foursome high five him after his tee shot. They hadn't cheered like banshees so I knew Jeff's shot wasn't a hole-in-one.

Jeff Grafton III walked straight toward me and stopped. So there he stood on the grass, looking down on me like some criminal court judge.

"You know, this reminds me of the time I was in that deep fescue and it took me five shots to get out of the crap. You remember that, Mikey?"

"Sure, Jeff."

"You remember what you said to me?"

"Ah. No. Not at the moment."

Manni and George, both dressed in black pants and black shirts, positioned themselves beside Jeff and stared down at me like Supreme Court judges.

"I said, 'I'll take the fifth.'" Jeff laughed, pointed at his chest and said, "Lawyer talk."

"Yep, it is lawyer talk." I had to agree. "Or whereas, most legalese from lawyers, about the party of the first part, is bullshit."

"If you ask me, you don't look ta be in any kind of perfect position, Michael," Manni advised. "You might wanta be careful what you say." Then he backhanded George's arm.

George scratched his head. "Jesus, Mikey, if I was you I'd be wearing a helmet."

"Probably no room in his golf bag. What with all those extra clubs he carries." Manni shook his head. "Somebody outa have given you a helmet." He elbowed George and the two of them walked toward the green.

Jeff grinned, rocked back on his heels, and I thought he was going to launch into opening arguments before a jury of one, but apparently he has been thinking about this line ever since he approached the pond. "Jeepers, Mikey, why didn't you just take an unplayable lie?" Jeff hooted, snickered and slapped his thigh.

"I'll take the fifth on that, Jeff. But, Jeff, I could use a good defence lawyer, to help me get out of this mess."

"You tell me, the party of the first part, that I'm speaking bullshit and then you want me to defend you? You don't need a lawyer, Mikey. Looks to me like you need a 'get out of jail' card." He chuckled at that one and walked to the green, yelling at his playing partners, "I want to put that birdie putt in the hole. Don't touch my ball."

My mouth had kick started long before my brain worked through what to say to Jeff. Maybe I should have appealed to their sense of justice. I made a real gaffe by telling Jeff he was full of bullshit. But he is a lawyer.

Don't get me started about lawyers. I don't even want to think about what I'd like to do to some of the lawyers I know. You know why God created Satan and lawyers; so He wouldn't have to take all the blame.

I groaned. The surface of the pond responded with a ripple coasting out from my heaving gasping chest. At least six foursomes had played through and I should have learned by now that the best action is to declare the unplayable rule right away and move on. I should have moved on as quietly as the ripples rolled toward the bulrushes behind me and toward the clipped grass at the pond's edge in front of me.

From this angle the cliff that is the 17th tee couldn't look more like Mount Everest than it does right now.

Chapter 8

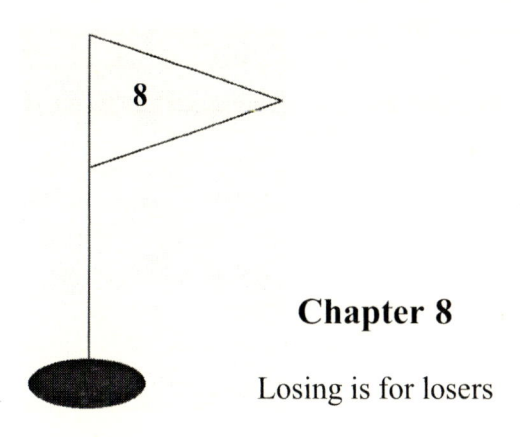

Losing is for losers

Looking up at the 17th tee, I feel as if this pond is more than five-foot deep, but exists at the bottom of a gorge and I have to climb higher than I ever had before. The peak feels insurmountable. I might as well be in the Niagara gorge, trying to climb up the Horseshoe Falls with its torrent of water rushing over me.

A couple of years ago someone came to work with colourful optical illusions; when you stare at some of those crazy patterns long enough, a hidden message starts to take form. At the time I was caught up in the puzzling consequences of locating the missing funds and didn't pay a lot of attention to the staring contests of the workforce. I was staring at the list of numbers that didn't add up and wondering why my boss would risk the anger of his staff when they found out profits were down because he and others had 'borrowed' cash from the business coffers. While my co-workers were playing optical illusion games, I tried to solve puzzles of a different nature.

The biggest puzzle was how to keep my job and report the greed of those above me. In my spare time, at home, late at night, I dug through the Internet for any information about protections for the 'whistleblower.' Our neighbours to the south were appreciative of insiders divulging corporate digressions, but in Canada there wasn't any protection for tattlers. Granted, I resented that my boss and his bosses spent corporate funds on their private yachts, residences, memberships at exclusively expensive golf courses and the BMWs they drove to get to their midweek golf games. I suffered in silence for a long time, and concealed my distaste for their thievery. For every dime they spent of the corporate profits, which show up as expenses on the balance sheet, employees receive less as bonus payouts. It wasn't just my bonus that was ripped out of my pocket before it landed, but all of us were shortchanged. And then they had the nerve to drive a brand new BMW Z30, 'baby Z', to the office. When I decided to outline my research to my boss and see what he would do about the transgressions, I thought I was taking the righteous route. But then when I opened the envelope with my bonus payment, I honestly believed that all the employees had received their bonus payments, too.

In the business world no one is supposed to talk about how much money one earns, as if it is a bad thing to be paid for services rendered, but my mother taught me to always thank those who gave gifts. So I respectfully entered my boss's office to thank him for the approval of bonus payments.

He looked up at me as if I was a crazy man and without whispering said clearly so his voice would carry forth out to the cubicle world, "There are no bonus payments this year. No profits."

I showed him my deposit record and he scratched his head, muttered something incomprehensible and said he'd look into it. "You shouldn't talk about this."

So I waited and wondered if I would have to repay the bonus.

A couple of weeks went by and I decided he was probably right, that I shouldn't talk about my receiving a bonus.

Then I was invited to play golf with the bosses at their exclusive private club and thought that maybe my climb up the ladder of success would start with my golf game in their presence. I thought my future was assured. My skills were more than just decent. I was excited to be part of the higher echelon of the corporate world. This was like a stairway to heaven. Driving in through the stone arched entranceway to their flower bordered, white washed, brick lined concrete driveway, I believed I was entering heaven. I was going to play golf on the lush, manicured fairways of the most exclusive golf course in the GTA.

A greeter on an electric cart came to get my clubs and informed me that I would be assigned a locker in the gentlemen's locker room where I was allowed to put my shoes on and that I must use the locker room for such a private activity. Because I was a guest and not a paid up member, I guess they expected to see holes in my socks, should I commit the crass activity of changing my shoes at the trunk of my car. Whatever.

As my boss and I walked from the locker room up the stairs to the pro shop, he whispered, "The boss never hits from behind a tree, always sets up his shots on the fairways. He's got a permanent 'get out of jail' card." My boss went on. "So if you're smart you won't mention his playing winter rules. If he tells you that he shot a five on a hole and not the seven that you may or may not witness, don't question it."

I was warned. There were rules. So not only did the president cheat on the corporate financial statement, he also cheated at golf. And this was obviously going to be their way of testing my integrity.

"You're the accountant, Michael," the senior executive of the group told me. "So you get to keep score."

I was in a serious quandary. All three of them cheated. At least one of them gave me the wrong score on every hole, and since I'm the better golfer I had the better game going. But they resented my beating them on the first three holes. From the intensity of their glares, I realised that if I beat them at golf, I wouldn't be welcomed in their elite group. So as they told me lower scores than they should have, I announced higher scores than I actually shot. Unfortunately, the third of the three executives had to correct me on the fifth hole, so I had to come up with some ways to miss hit shots and give them some memorable duffer-style drives, sloppy sand shots and wicked slices. They took great pleasure at reliving my hilarious attempts at scrambling for bogey. By the twelfth hole, I was more than a little annoyed at their reincarnated descriptions of how I screwed up the last hole.

"What's throwing me off my game is the way you kick up a little dust before you hit out of the trees. How all your balls are Titleist, and the last one you lost in the rough was under Edward's foot, but miraculously you found the ball that dropped from your pocket."

That shut them up. And I, very soon after that glorious day at that GTA exclusive golf club, received a warning letter from the Human Resources department. "It has come to our attention that sarcastic comments are not welcome. If you or anyone of your staff are exhibiting sarcasm, please refrain from doing so. A copy of this letter will go in your personnel file."

I wasn't surprised that I never received another invitation to play golf with them. Shortly after that I received the layoff notice. Profits were down, money was tight, they were downsizing and I was on the list to leave the glorious and hallowed halls of the company. I was escorted out. And I was too late to blow the whistle on how the executives had ripped off the corporate coffers. If I went to Revenue Canada after my layoff, they and Revenue Canada would think I just wanted revenge.

That same week, I received a letter from the handicap committee at my own club.

>Dear Michael Blaine:
>
>After reviewing your scoring record, the Men's Section Handicap Committee of CrossCreek Golf and Country Club has determined that your RCGA handicap factor does not accurately reflect your potential playing ability. We have concluded that your failure to post scores, and your posting of erroneous scores, has produced a handicap factor that is not accurate.
>
>In the interest of fair play, the Handicap Committee is going to modify your RCGA handicap factor in accordance with Section 8-4 of the "RCGA Handicap System" manual. Your RCGA handicap factor will become 10. Before the adjustment becomes effective, you may appeal to the Handicap Committee either by letter or in person by August 4.

If the Committee does not hear from you, or determines that the reasons for modification are still valid, the modified handicap factor will become effective on August 5.

The Handicap Committee will review this adjustment regularly to determine if your handicap factor should revert to the normal RCGA handicap formula computation. In the meantime, continue to post all of your scores and observe all aspects of the RCGA Handicap System.

Sincerely,

Handicap Chairman

Everyone hated the Handicap Chairman. But I learned my lesson. I would never again shoot an eighty-two and enter a eighty-five in the computer score tracking system. If I need to keep my handicap up, I'll shoot the appropriate score and let the bean counters reincarnate my missed shots. If I know how to correct a slice, then I sure as hell ought to know how to hit a slice and put my ball into trees, sand traps, and fescue and jump my gross score beyond belief. I'll show them that I know the numbers game better than anyone. I lost a lot of money that year; my salary, my game was shot to hell and I paid off debts. Living idly on employment insurance, I had time to perfect my trick shots: how to get into trouble.

But now, as my visions of the past become misty-eyed images, and my view of the October weeds on the cliff side of the 17th tee blend into hues of thistle purple, musty orange, blood red crow-chewed berries, I desperately hope the next foursome on the tee will see me, take pity and haul me out of this mess.

At the top of the cliff I can see the nose of a cart. Because of glare on the windshield I can't make out who is in the cart. I blink as rapidly as I can to clear away the mist in my eyes, and squinted up at the elevated tee. The foursome appeared at the edge and one man pointed. His right arm extended, swooped as if offering a feast to an honoured guest. His lean form and red shirt, and the way he flexed his knees are dead giveaway indicators that the captain of this foursome is Dr. Willis Nelson.

I'd seen Willie in the coffee shop before I teed off and know that his honoured guest is none other than Arthur Pearson, the chairman of the board of one of the most profitable, top fifty employers in the greater Toronto area. Arthur Pearson is very nearly the Canadian equivalent to Donald Trump, prestigious resident of the US of A. I don't know how many times I tried to arrange meetings with Arthur Pearson's Human Resources department, his Chief Financial Officer and any one else who might network my way into a job interview with Arthur Pearson and company. I had even tried talking to Dr. Nelson about his prestigious friend.

Unfortunately, Dr. Nelson is a psychologist who specialises in behaviour modification and earned his degree by jabbing electrodes into rat brains and watching them press buttons to receive either shocks or food. As a sideline he raised rats that he sold to laboratories. He is personally responsible for most of the obese rodents in North America. After he received his doctorate degree, he decided that corporate work would fatten up his personal bank account a lot faster than social service work. He became a consultant, advising corporations about how to test potential employees, compensate or discipline employees. Through that work he became an expert at downsizing and owned a business that counselled departing employees on how to find another job. Apparently, he originally planned to be a psychiatrist but couldn't get into medical school. And when he was studying clinical psychology, couldn't stand working with patients that had severe psychosis. He is a psychologist who doesn't like to work with nuts. Besides, eccentrics paid more for his services since they were crazy rich people, whereas the average schizophrenic, because his or her hallucinations took on different flights of fancy, couldn't hold down a job and wouldn't be able to pay for the psychologist's services.

Still, Dr. Nelson claims to have some pretty good aptitude tests that could, for a fee, guide the unemployed to find his or her true worth and true calling. The last time I was unemployed I asked Dr. Nelson about the testing that he does, and with his delusions of grandeur, believing he could do some behaviour modification or psychiatric analysis on me, and through the grapevine he knew that I was wallowing in the mess of a potential divorce, he thought I wanted counselling. He tried to counsel me and blamed my lack of a job on some Jungian philosophy. My failure, he said, was because in my ancestral background my relatives were tradesmen, not executives, and I should return to my roots. Granted, he was pretty drunk at that moment, but I didn't need some ancient philosophical argument about group memory, when what I needed was a job interview. I didn't want to get back to my roots. If I hadn't been so inebriated I might have planted him next to some roots.

In the light of day I forgave his insult and contemplated booking an appointment for occupational testing with Dr. Nelson, but only to convince him I am a forthright kind of employee. At that time, I couldn't afford the two hundred bucks an hour so I didn't officially ask for an appointment. Besides, I thought he was a bit nuttier than I am and what kind of a recommendation would that be? But now, seeing as how he's coming down the tarmac path, and seeing as how psychologists are supposed to be compassionate, if anyone is going to rescue me, I thought Dr. Willis Nelson would.

In contrast to that opportunity, Arthur Pearson was riding shotgun on the cart and I don't particularly want the coveted employer to know why I've been tossed into the pond. This situation won't be much of a reference for a job, either.

Seeing as how I'm very nearly at the bottom of the barrel and desperate to get out of this watery grave, I opted to entice Dr. Nelson over to the pond. Little known fact about him is that he is a bird-watcher. Birds and fighter jets and pretty well anything else that flew. Armed with that knowledge, I drew his attention the only way I could. I buried my face in the surface and shook my head, sqwacked like a prehistoric water demon, bumped my shoulders and elbows as much as I could, and know that the ruckus in the water that probably looked like an injured Canada goose would entice Dr. Nelson to the edge of the pond.

Hopefully Arthur Pearson will appreciate the creative, out-of-the box thinking that I'm demonstrating. I assume Arthur Pearson will live up to his charitable standards.

When I lift my face, water dripped down from my forehead, and I shook my head like a dog shaking off rain. Sure enough, Dr. Nelson and his guest came for a ride to the side of the pond. And right up beside his cart, Cyril MacMirsh and Lloyd MacInnis, two of our seriously Scottish members, stopped by the pond, too.

"Hey, doc. Great day for a golf game," I called out and grinned. "Welcome to CrossCreek, Mr. Pearson."

Arthur Pearson laughed.

Cyril bellowed from the other cart. "Are ye up a creek without a paddle, Mikey?"

"No task is insurmountable, Mikey. Some people never ask for help." Lloyd pulled himself up and out of the driver's seat.

Dr. Nelson leaned out the side of the cart and said in a tone that could have been confidential, "You know, Mikey, some people know when they need hydrotherapy. Did you ask for this treatment?"

"He asked for it all right. That's a little CrossCreak hydrotherapy," Cyril added and punched his fist out to nudge Dr. Nelson's arm and laughed like a demon.

"Well, Cyril, some people hear voices from unknown sources. Some build castles in the sky," Dr. Nelson pontificated.

"And psychologists shoot holes in the castle walls," Arthur Pearson offered in way of a joke.

"What you need, Michael, is a little behaviour modification."

"What I need, Dr. Nelson, is someone to pull me out of this pond. That would go along way toward modifying my current situation. I don't think this is a job for a Newfie Viking analyst, Dr. Nelson," I suggested, referring back to when he claimed to be a direct descendant from the Vikings who landed on Newfoundland.

Mr. Pearson laughed like a snorting pig. "Willis, are you a Newfie? No wonder you have some wild ideas about corporate ethics." Everyone stared at Mr. Pearson's snorting laugh. "Newfie Vikings ought to know how to build a boat that floats."

Arthur Pearson chuckled and snorted. "You sure don't know how to float my boat. Did I tell you I'm being investigated by the Ontario Securities Commission?" Arthur punched Dr. Nelson's arm. "I can't pay your bill, Doctor Newfie Viking. That's a good one."

Everyone was definitely shocked by Arthur Pearson's admission that he is being investigated. And obviously Dr. Nelson wasn't happy about hearing that his invoices wouldn't be paid.

"What's the matter, Willis? Can't you handle the truth?" Pearson laughed louder. "You can't handle the truth. Love that line. Jack Nicholson really delivered that one."

Dr. Nelson stood up beside the cart. "Michael, let me know if you have any recurring nightmares. Call me for an appointment. I'll make sure you get one. A recurring nightmare! I do know how to insert electrodes into rats."

Both drivers pressed the reverse button and the carts beeped as they backed away.

"Doc, I don't think he needs a psychologist. I think he needs a row boat," Cyril yelled as they drove back to the tarmac path

"One with holes in it, like his head," Lloyd called out as the cart carried him away.

I don't know exactly what I'd done to those two yahoo duffers, but they weren't very sympathetic and Dr. Nelson was a total disappointment. He, who should have expressed some sympathy for my plight, offered none whatsoever. I'm definitely a loser in their eyes. Their eyes only. Not mine. I'm not a loser. I'm depressed.

Considering the psychologist had been no help at all and his buddies are all nuts, I'm even more depressed. Whatever the newspapers had said about Arthur Pearson and his excessive compassion are just a bunch of lies. There's no way I wanted to work for him. Not now that he's being investigated by the OSC.

I'm lucky that I'd never landed a job with him. I'd sure as shooting be in the Don jail for fudging the books and claiming to just be following orders, which doesn't hold any water anymore. If a Marine can't use that excuse, as evidenced by the verdict in *A Few Good Men*, then what's a lowly accountant to claim as an excuse?

Chapter 9

Get out of jail card

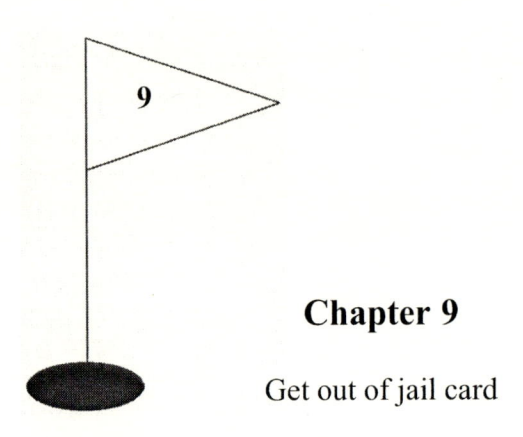

I need a get out of jail card. Or as Cyril put it, a row boat. The only thing I can do is squawk like that prehistoric goose, so I let out another screech and hope I've timed it right to ruin the psychologist's putt on the 17th green behind me. All I heard in return was silence and no one appeared on the ridge that is the 17th tee.

With nothing else to do, I thought about all the times I've been in jail. In civilian life, out on the streets, I've only been in jail once. Late one night I stole Mom's car. I was fifteen and wanted to cruise around with my buddies, so that summer night after eleven, after Mom and Dad went to bed, I sneaked out of the house, put the car in neutral and pushed it out of the sloping driveway. The only sound was the rubber tires kissing the pavement. I cranked the key and nearly jumped out of my skin at the blast of sound. I looked over my shoulder to see if they heard the sound and turned on the light in their bedroom to see who was revving the engine in the neighbourhood. The windows stayed dark. Revving the engine was an accident. My foot slipped. An hour later, my friends and I were bored to tears. Nothing happened in Millartown after midnight. Population ten thousand and all ten thousand, minus the four of us, were asleep. The guys opted to go home and I cruised home just in time to see Dad talking to two cops at a patrol car in the driveway.

Mom and Dad believed in consequences. So they let the cops arrest me and toss me in the drunk tank at the local jail. Fortunately, and considering it was a Tuesday night, the drunk tank wasn't occupied, but the remnants of previous residents lingered like an unflushed sewer and overheated sweatshop.

Dad picked me up in the morning and I swore I would burn the clothes on my back and never steal his car again. That was the only time I was ever in real jail.

But I've been 'in jail' a million times on the golf course. To a golfer, 'in jail' is finding the misdirected golf ball in the middle of trees. As I look from the ball to the green or fairway, the tree trunks look like the bars of a jail cell. Getting out of that jail is like threading a needle. The shooter has to choose the best path, usually through the widest gap between tree trunks, which may take the ball to the fairway or forward toward the green. The best choice may be to go backwards so the next shot is a clean hit to the green. There is no option to go up and over a tree with a lofted club. The golf ball must thread the needle between tree trunks.

I've made this shot so often, I can do it in my sleep. It's clearly a matter of geometry, physics, knowing the angles of the flight and where I want the face of the club to hit the ball to give me a direct line to the safest spot. Depending on the distance the ball has to travel to get out of jail, I select a nine iron or a five iron. A nine iron has loft so if the distance is only fifty yards or less, I'll use that club and close down the club face, set the ball back in my stance, hit down on and through the ball, keeping the club head low. Low back swing, low follow through. If the distance is more than fifty yards, I'll use my five iron and give the ball enough power to skitter through the trees and long grass. The line of flight is perpendicular to the bottom edge of the club. The follow through has to be straight along this flight path. Focusing on that technique, I can get out of jail every time.

A straight path. At the moment, with my hair dripping wet and in a locked down, tied down, weighted down position in the pond, getting out of this type of confinement will probably involve draining the pond. I need to convince the golfers yet to come by that what I need and want is a sump pump, a tow truck and a winch to drag my sorry being out of this bulrush bordered muck.

I still don't see anyone on the 17th tee and let out another prehistoric screeching squawk. As luck prevailed, the only attention I drew is from Kaida.

Kaida is a Border Collie who guards our ponds from the invading hordes of Canada geese. In the spring before the geese set up housekeeping, Kaida herds them, rounds them up and chases them into terrified flight. Our fairways and, in particular, the 17th green is a lot cleaner since Kaida came to rule their roosts.

He's an intelligent dog but once his charging rampages scatter the Canada geese to other landscapes, there isn't a lot for him to do. He finds other activities to keep him occupied. He especially likes to play fetch and I've seen him pick up a pine cone, drop it at the feet of a groundskeeper, then bounce back, lower his head and wait for the staff member to toss the pine cone for Kaida to fetch. Kaida knows enough not to chase flying golf balls, stays off the greens and fairways unless escorted by the grounds keeping staff on a mission to clear the property of marauding geese. Kaida whiles away his days playing fetch.

In response to my squawking goose imitation, Kaida came down to the 17th pond, on a happy trot, and paced back and forth around the pond. Obviously my screeching squawking imitation of a stranded goose has caught his finely tuned hearing and now he's on the prowl to find the misdirected fowl. As I watch him pace back and forth and sniff the ground at the pond's edge, I wonder if he'd be at all useful in getting me out of the pond. As bright as he is, I don't know if he will do the Lassie trick and go and fetch Timmy or whoever cared that someone was in trouble. Kaida is smart, but is he as smart as Lassie?

What the hell.

"Kaida. Good boy."

His head came up and his nose aimed my way. His ears stood up and he stared.

"How ya doing, Kaida?"

With that he laid down, paws and nose pointed right at me.

"Hey, Kaida. Do something for me. Go and get help. Fetch me some friends."

Okay, so that isn't the brightest phrase in my vocabulary. Kaida heard the word 'fetch' and his back end hunched up, his head down and his tail flagged at the horizon. He bounced. He jogged. He hunched his head and shoulders down and then he prowled for something to play fetch with. Seconds later he came back to the edge of the pond with a two-foot long stick. He tossed it in the air and it dropped in the grass, just at the edge of the pond. Kaida picked it up, tossed his head up and opened his jaws. The stick flipped, landed in the water.

"Good boy. Kaida. Now go and get Jeff." Jeff is the greenskeeper who takes Kaida out on goose chasing rounds. "Where's Jeff? Go get Jeff. Good boy, Kaida. Get Jeff."

I figure if I can get Jeff's attention, he might drag me out of the pond. "Go get Jeff, Kaida. Where's Jeff?"

Kaida cocked his head. His ears twitched. He looked down at the floating stick, looked at me then hunched down again and attempted to push the stick toward me.

"Get Jeff. Get Jeff," I said. "Good boy."

Kaida looked around, over his shoulder toward the clubhouse.

"Go find Jeff. Find Jeff. Bring him here. Good boy, Kaida."

I honestly believe I'm getting through to the dog when he turned and headed toward the clubhouse.

"Thata boy. Good dog."

Then Kaida faced me again, hunched down again, and with huge brown eyes and whimpers, begged me to toss the stick for him.

"Kaida! Get Jeff!"

Maybe 'Get Jeff,' sounds like 'fetch.' Next thing I know, Kaida ran full tilt at me and dove over the edge of the pond. His front paws pointed and he made a perfect belly flop onto the brown water. He swam around for a bit, grabbed the floating stick and brought it to me.

"Good boy, Kaida. Real good."

So here we are, nose to nose. My hands are tied. He nudged the stick closer to my chin. As much as I want to toss the freaking stick for him, I can't.

"Get Jeff. Kaida, get Jeff," I whispered.

He whimpered.

I whimpered.

At that moment I recognized that, in fact, misery does not love company.

He stared at me, paddled around, nudged the stick, sneezed, and fluffed pond water at my face.

"Yeah. I know. I'd like to get out of here, too. Here's the story, Kaida."

What the hell. So far none of the golfers have listened to me today.

"You go and get Jeff and tomorrow I'll bring you a T-bone steak. I promise." I can only hope Kaida, captain of the goose-chasing brigade, will succumb to a bribe. "Remember that terrific bone I brought you last month? Remember that chew toy I gave you? Well, Kaida, now is the time for payback. Go GET JEFF."

Just like Lassie he barked.

"Good boy."

He paddled to the edge of the pond and I watched him struggle to get out. He tried half a dozen places but the edge was too high.

I pointed with the only thing I could point with. My head. "Over there, Kaida. Try there."

He paddled. He swam. He barked and he scrambled up the edge of the pond near the cart path. Then he ran along the edge, barking and proclaiming his success. He stood and shook off his excess water.

"Good boy! Well done, Kaida!"

He started trotting up toward the clubhouse, shaking a back leg every few paces.

"Go get 'em, Kaida!"

The pause and the look he gave me over his shoulder reminds me of one of my wife's responses when I asked her for some walking around cash. She was none too happy to be supporting me while I searched for employment.

I looked up to the 17th tee and figured by the gap between playing groups that the next foursome is way behind in recommended speed of play. In my mind I searched through the tee off time sheet for the day and pretty much calculated that the next group I'll face will be Jake and the Fat Man, and Billy Banterson.

Jake was a cop and the Fat Man was Ian Butcher, the fattest member of our club, and Billy Banterson was a skinny, hunched over man.

I started to count on Jake to lead my rescue team. Jake is a cop. A good cop, and he wouldn't let anyone die. He'll get me out of this mess.

Sure enough, the group eventually appeared at the top of the cliff and eyed the flag on the green behind me. My view of the three of them standing side by side is like looking at the Toronto City Hall with the two curved skinny towers and the middle short, squat flying saucer shaped object. The fourth member of their group is about half the height of Ian Butcher but in proportion, just as round. That had to be Ian's son, John.

I started to think that John might be my best hope yet. I taught him how to hit a shot out of tree-jail. I taught him sand shots. I've played golf with him a dozen times on Junior Tuesdays. These fathers, Jake, Ian, and Billy, wouldn't be obnoxious to me in front of the twelve-year-old John Butcher. They'd live up to expectations and rescue me right away.

Had to.

All four of them hit pretty decent shots. Not one ball landed in the pond or even short of the pond, so the likelihood of one or more of them facing me to drop a ball and hit from the tee side of the pond was over.

Jake came marching down the path like a man on a mission. He turned and called back up to the tee, "Hurry up. We're way behind! Get a move on!"

Ian and his offspring came down the hill riding in a cart. Driving and rocking back and forth the kid, John, hooted like a baboon. I've told him a dozen times not to do that. The kid shouldn't be riding in a cart, anyway. He should be walking and maybe lose a hundred or so of the excess weight he heaves around. Like a drunk was at the wheel, the cart careened back and forth on the path, scraped against the dried up raspberry bushes and prickly weeds, bounced toward the down side, lost a wheel over the edge of the tarmac, and switched back to the thistles. If the kid hadn't been yelling and hooting, Jake wouldn't have known he was the target of an out of control hit and run driver.

Jake started to run, changed direction like a quarterback carrying the touchdown ball. His bag bounced against his back, then he dove off the path toward the cliff side of the path and lost his golf bag. The bag stood up for a second, like a stupid white hunter facing two elephants charging on an electric golf car.

The crash sent the golf bag flying, clubs popped out, flew like batons tossed in the air by the Dallas Cowboys cheerleaders entertaining the fans.

John and Ian, on the cart, held on for their lives. Then the cart disappeared from my view. By the sound of the next piece of noise they must have crashed into the small wooden bridge over the creek that drained overflow out of my pond.

I saw Jake crawl out of the weeds like some jungle guerrilla warfare sniper and he has to be about that mad. Even from my distance I can see how red in the face he is. He eyed the disaster at the bridge, which couldn't have been that bad, because instead of trying to rescue the fat man and his Pillsbury doughboy son, Jake picked up his clubs and yanked weeds from his hair. He stayed silent. Not one sound came out of him as he collected his scattered clubs, slammed them one at time back in his bag, and hoisted the bag over his shoulder.

With a glare at the crazed golf cart accident victims he screeched, "I've had it with you two. I'm out of here." Jake headed directly across the front of the pond to the path up the hill toward the clubhouse.

Billy Banterson, on his own cart, came down the path from the 17th tee with his foot on the brake, and effectively made the gears howl in agony. "You guys okay? Anyone hurt?"

Too soon, he's gone from my view. Even if I want to yell to them, they're out of range and besides, my throat hurts like hell. Afraid that John Butcher, the kid driving the cart, would hit Jake, the cop, I tried to scream at Jake to get out of the way, but not one sound came out of me. I've strained my vocal chords and since I have no voice to call out to the cop as he followed Kaida's path up to the clubhouse, I've probably missed my best chance of getting out of this watery jail and being rescued anytime soon. Not by that cop. He'll be gone for the rest of the year.

I just hope I'm not still in the pond when he comes back in the spring.

Chapter 10

Anger management

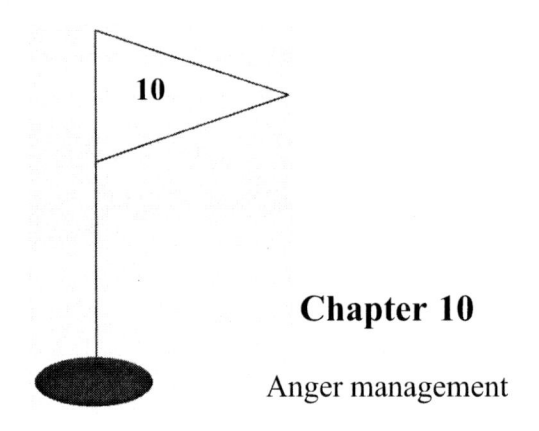

Everyone knows that Jake has a temper, but he's never exploded at the club. He's managed to control his anger. This isn't the first time he's walked off the course because of some idiotic act by a playing partner. I suppose it is his police academy training or just that he knows that if he really lost his temper he could uproot trees. I doubt he has attended leadership courses like I have.

One company I worked for was very progressive and offered leadership courses at the office. Middle managers, like myself, were invited to attend courses on 'effecting change,' 'overcoming objections,' 'involving your subordinates in decision-making,' and 'anger management.' I wanted to be an executive and knew that if I took those seminars it would look good in the eyes of my boss and I'd possibly learn something. I learned a lot more than I expected.

I learned how to effect change and set goals. I learned how to turn pessimism into optimism, I learned how to let the people who worked for me think they were making decisions. And I learned about anger management.

For a well-placed bet in a game of golf, all of these were especially useful to know.

Let me cite examples. Effecting change in the golf swing requires setting goals, and working toward that goal. I took lessons and I hung around the driving range and practised my chipping and putting.

Every time I've had a negative thought, like 'oh no, I'll never hit over that pond,' I'll change that thought to 'Oh good! A challenge. Everyone likes a challenge. It feels so good when you beat the challenge.'

As for letting subordinates believe they were making decisions, every time I wanted to place a bet, I came up with ways to let the guys ask me first. I'd let them talk me into betting. They believed it was their idea.

And I learned an awful lot in the anger management course.

In that seminar I learned that expressing anger looks stupid. I know guys that have tossed their golf club in a pond out of sheer anger and frustration. One golfer tossed his sand wedge into the creek behind the 17th green and then needed it when he got to the eighteenth greenside bunker.

He looked pretty sily, after wading into the creek and arriving at the deck of the club dripping wet and no club in his hands. We all had a good laugh at his expense. He just got madder and madder and his face turned red and he broke his hand when he slammed his fist into the deck railing. He was out one sand wedge and then sported a cast for the rest of the summer. I play golf with another golfer who, when he has one bad hole, is furious for the next two holes, which he then plays badly and pouts or storms off and simply has to pay off his debts. If I made a bet with him and he's winning (and I'm short of cash), I can change that around by making him miss a shot, and watch him get angry.

Anger management in my house took some pretty extensive planning. There was a time when the marriage was pretty good and for some reason we were playing nooky on the bed more often. Then one of the sports casters on the TSN, the sports channel, made some wiseass remark that athletes in training shouldn't have sex the night before a major event.

So here's what I did. I tried telling my wife I was 'in training' and couldn't afford to expend energy before the club championship. She didn't believe it. So then I managed to have an argument with her the night before important and valuable rounds of golf and she'd be so annoyed she would refuse any nooky I then offered. She'd sleep badly. I'd sleep like a baby and play my A game the next day. How's that for anger management?

There haven't been any players on the 17th tee in a while. I'm still hoping that Freddy will come out from the clubhouse and pull my sorry and soggy mess from the pond, but at least three groups had played the 17th since Freddy promised to come back. I calculated that he was just about finished his second beer. Since I know that Freddy doesn't drink a lot, I figure he'll be out my way pretty soon. And I'm getting antsy.

It was all a joke, to be tied to my golf bag and cart and tossed in the pond, but I've been here for at least two hours. The sun is beating down on my head and if I was tied to a stake in the middle of a desert, I would be suffering dehydration by now. But I'm in a pond. Dehydration was out of the question. The sun drilling into my head is another matter. And the sun beating on the pond, warming the water is almost a guarantee that I won't freeze to death. But it is no joke that the pond was starting to smell.

I'm more than antsy. In fact, I'm getting angry. Really angry.

In all my summers of laying bets, winning and losing, I didn't win that much. Hell, I haven't paid off the house yet. So the guys can't be that mad at me. They should know how to manage their anger and not hold grudges. Hell, I haven't even paid the last bill from my divorce lawyer. At the rate he's delaying things, I'm prepared to call another lawyer and not pay the first. Let him sue me.

Finally, a foursome has arrived on the 17th tee and as every group does, they stood at the cliff edge and eyed the flag. I know right off that one of them is Al Kazan.

Al is one of the best actors on and off the golf course. He's a salesman and claims to be related to that famous stage and film director Elia Kazan. You know the one. The one who gave a list of Hollywood actors who were members of the communist party to the committee on un-American activities, back when McCarthyism was the scourge of the decade.

Al claimed that he's such a good salesman, he could act his way out of an objectionable situation. He always claims that if a sale doesn't happen today, it will happen tomorrow. There is no point in being angry because that will just waste energy that he could otherwise use to make that sale tomorrow. Al Kazan is an inspiration. He is always an optimist. Never angry. Never seems to hold a grudge. He'd just smiled his way to sale after sale, profit begets profit. Anger never begets anything.

Well, I have to be-get my butt out of the pond and I figure, if anyone would, Al would help me out. Al Kazan is the man.

All four of the guys made decent shots over the pond and I held off calling out to them until they were within calling distance. So as they strolled down the tarmac cart path, intensely listening to one of Al's jokes, I waited until they were on level ground.

"Hey, Al."

Man, they froze and started looking around. None of them replied or even spoke.

Then they started walking again; obviously, each man is afraid to admit he heard a voice calling from beyond the bulrushes.

"Al, it's me," I said calmly.

Al stopped, looked up, looked to his right, turned and looked back at the 17th tee cliff. I followed his stare and guess what? Up there on the cliff is a golfer who is standing there with his arms spread out like he's hanging on a cross. Oh, man. That image is likely going to ruin my plan to ask Al Kazan to pull me out of the pond.

"No. Al, over here," I whispered again but a little louder this time.

Al is a huge fan of Bill Cosby and God. Al particularly likes Bill Cosby's monologue about when God calls out to him. Al and his wife regularly watch that television show, *Touched by an Angel*. Al never plays golf on Sunday morning. Al goes to church every Sunday. Al bought a copy of George Burn's movie *Oh God*. If anyone is going to help me, it would be Al Kazan.

So here I am, up to my neck in swamp water calling out from the bulrushes with a gentle request and some Jesus figure is on the cliff.

Al is between us.

Al and I are both staring up at the cliff where the golfer on the cliff now started singing gospel songs.

I looked at Al.

His knees began to quake.

"Al, I'm over here. Forget him."

Al's body started to shake.

"Al, that's just George Campbell," Ronny Post called out from the green. "He's in that musical *Godspell* next month. You know that amateur production in Brampton. Come on, Al," Ronny Post yelled to Al from the green side of the pond. "Come on!"

"No. Al, come here," I beckoned.

Al jerked his head toward me.

The cliff top gospel singer belted out "OH YEAAAAAH!"

I watched in horror as the Archangel with a golf ball in one hand, a nine iron in the other, pointed the club down at Al and yelled, "Al Kazan! YOU THE MAN!"

Al stared up at the cliff, and then as his head went farther back, he fell backwards. Flat out fainted.

"GEESH, Al. Ya gotta finish the game. You got a hole-in-one on the third hole. Come on, Al!" Ronny Post ran toward Al, and I, in the pond, am paralytic.

I'm terrified that Al would die right there and my whispering to him from the bulrushes gave him a heart attack. Since I'm bound by bungie cords to my golf bag, I know that I am the least of that foursome's worries; I had to keep my mouth shut.

At that point, I think I wet my pants, but being in the middle of a pond, who would know? Besides, it's a tiny matter compared with the scene of Al Kazan laying at the side of the cart path, and three guys hovering around him, the Godspell singer still yelling and pointing like Moses from the mount.

If I wasn't afraid of drowning, I might have fainted at that scene too.

You'll be happy to know that Al revived, sat up, and was pulled up to his feet. The gospel singer on the cliff was still waving his arms and dancing like an Indian. I could hear Al ask Ronny, "Indians don't believe in God, do they?"

Ronny Post said, "That was just George Campbell. You know what a goof he is."

"Come on, Al. You have to finish the game and then we *ALL* get a free drink. Hole-in-one! A HOLE-IN-ONE! Al, ya gotta finish the game," one of Al's playing partners yelled as he dragged Al's golf pull cart toward the green.

"Oh, yeah." Al grinned and peered at the bulrushes.

"YOU THE MAN!" George yelled from the cliff, and pranced around like a Navaho rain dance warrior.

Al turned and waved at the cliff. "I got a hole-in-one! ME!" Then he marched along as if he hadn't fainted at all.

"YOU THE MAN!" George Campbell bellowed from the cliff.

I groaned.

I don't know if they heard me or not. I groaned because I knew that when Al Kazan arrives at the clubhouse and signs the bar tab for the hole-in-one free drinks, the guys will have a free drink and begin the en-mass celebration. Al Kazan has never had a hole-in-one. I've never had a hole-in-one. For a dedicated golfer, it's like winning the lottery. No wonder he fainted. For a religious man, hearing whispers from the bulrushes, gospel singing from a dancing Indian on the cliff and a hole-in-one, all in one day, his adrenaline has to be jumping all over the map. And no wonder he revived. A hole-in-one doesn't officially count unless all eighteen holes are played.

A hole-in-one? And he had to do it today?

I'm stuck in the pond, and knowing that the guys will be celebrating Al's hole-in-one with drinks for all, I'm getting even madder.

I'm going to be in the pond longer than the Loch Ness monster.

Chapter 11

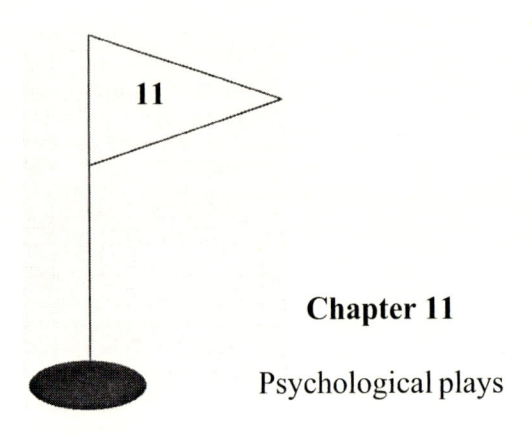

Psychological plays

George, the gospel singer, rain dancer warrior on the tee was getting ready to hit his shot. I don't have to worry about George hitting his shot into the pond. Standing near him though is Dr. Neville Decorte, a psycho psychotherapist, who is always giving advice, pontificating about bad behaviour, putting excessive emphasis on Freudian analysis, and most of us just think he's an evangelist for an outdated fad.

Who in their right mind can believe that women envy men for an appendage that doesn't always work on command and sometimes tries to work at inappropriate times? But we do sort of like Neville's theory about why men are so passionate about golf. How many men can say, 'Yep, I got it in the hole eighteen times in five hours."

George and Neville are a strange pairing, but do surprisingly well in two-ball match play or better ball tournaments. And they have had some of the strangest beer induced discussions on the deck after a round of golf. George is native Indian, from the six nations group in the Niagara peninsula. He was raised by his grandparents and claimed that his grandfather was a direct descendant of one of the tribal chiefs. Consequently, George knows all the myths and legends from his tribe. When he told us his grandmother died because "she saw the Bear Walker in her dreams," Dr. Neville's Decorte's first reaction was to ask, "Why, was the walker naked?"

George went into a long discourse about how in his tribal legends, the animal, the bear, is the symbol of death. Dr. Decorte tends to giggle about the bare bear.

George called Neville a woman who envies his own useless appendage. Neville took offense at that and called George a diluted road warrior on a throbbing Harley because his own appendage can't throb on command. The rest of us were in stitches, holding our guts and spewing beer from our mouths and noses as the two of them got deeper into the mythology of each other's beliefs. George is the one who declared Neville's adoration of Freud's theory of sexual envy, hysterical blindness and other nut cases as an outdated fad, as bad as betting on the Toronto Maple Leafs year after year. That got the rest of us up in arms and it led to a major discussion of the myths of the best players from thirty some years ago.

The next day there they were, Neville and George, teeing it up in a two-man best ball tournament.

Today, the third player in the foursome on the tee is Peter Mullen. Peter is one of my favourite suckers. Peter doesn't like betting on a game. But I can get more money out of a game with Peter than just about any other sucker at the course. Peter is the all-time winner of the most number of putts in a season.

I bet on his putts. When you think about it, it adds up nicely. There are eighteen holes, but how many golfers are there who can make eighteen or fewer putts in a round of golf? The aim is to do that, but it's almost impossible. "Regulation" is two putts per green. A great round is described as having under thirty putts per round. Peter is a sucker for every putting gadget, new style of putter, and new grip that ever was invented. He will plumb-bob a six inch putt and if he agrees to a-buck-bet, he'll miss the putt. I love Peter. He has the best selection of putters in his basement, lined up on the wall like a gun lover shows off his rifle collection. His wife commented that the putters must be mating in the basement and the species has a very short pregnancy.

As for betting on putts, I always read my opponent's putting line on the green. I know if he is right or left-handed. The scariest putt for right-handed players and the one they have the most trouble making is a putt that breaks left to right. Downhill putts with a left to right break are the most difficult for most right-handed golfers. And the opposite is true for left handed players. The odds are he won't make it.

I'll win the 'betcha can't make that' challenge nine times out of ten. But if his left foot moves back from his normal line up, then I don't bet. He's setting up to hit a slice. A slicing putt! Yes it works. It's still a tough shot to make, but the odds on winning that bet just dropped.

"Betcha can't make that." I'll put pressure on Peter. "Betcha a buck. Betcha a looney."

Guys that don't like to miss a four foot putt, and don't like to bet much at all, will bet a buck. But the odds are with me that they'll miss. A guy who has a long uphill putt and has short putted on all the greens, I'll bet that he can't get it to the hole. "Betcha won't get it to the hole."

I'll remind him that he's short putted on every green until now. Chances are, he'll get so tense he'll barely get it halfway up the hill or he'll over slam it and yank his stroke. And if he bangs the shot on his uphill putt, now he has a downhill putt. I'll bet him again. These kinds of penny ante challenge bets add up. I love Peter Mullen. He always believes in his new grip, his new putter, his new technique, and he always agrees to a buck-a-putt bet.

The fourth player to hit off the tee is Walter Graham. He is a short man with a Santa belly, light blue eyes, and a baldhead, and is one of the nicest men at the club. He's a lefty, didn't start to play golf until he was in his fifties but had coached baseball and hockey when he was younger. He's a retired self-made entrepreneur, who got into the sand and gravel business and then when he was hit with the golf bug, he donated sand and gravel to a few golf courses in the area in exchange for ownership shares. I heard he and his wife lived on the dividends those golf club shares paid annually. He kept the dividend paying shares in the good years and sold when the recession hit early in the nineties. He believed that golf was a leisure activity and people who were out of work couldn't afford to play golf.

If Walter were still in business, I'd learn how to drive a dump truck so I could work for him. One man he employed for twenty years weighed over three hundred pounds. Every year Walter had to have the driver's seat of the truck replaced because Harold ruined the springs. When Harold died, Walter paid for the funeral. He had to have a piano crate renovated to become a coffin and needed a fork lift truck to get the coffin from the funeral home to the back of the dump trunk for the procession to the cemetery, where a front end loader worked like an overhead crane to lift the coffin to the double wide grave. Walter paid for all of that. But I enjoyed Walter because he saw through my bets with Peter and then would agree with Peter. "Sure, Peter. I've seen your new putter work wonders. You can make this putt. Take the bet."

When Peter missed the putt, as he usually did, Walter twinkled his blue eyes at me and would say, "I didn't say the putter worked in Peter's hands."

Walter and Peter would laugh and off we'd go to the next hole. I'd make a couple of bucks on Peter's putting errors and double or nothing if he had more than three putts on any green.

Walter is one of those guys who just likes being on the course, likes being outdoors and likes sportsmanship in all things.

As they came down the hill from the tee to the green, the group behind them started yelling, "Hurry up! What's taking so long! Get your act in gear, guys!"

Walter stopped and looked back at those guys. "Patience. Patience. Just enjoy the day."

George came over to the edge of the pond and stared right at me, but as I was about to say something, he turned to Walter, Peter, and Neville and said, "Hey, Peter, it's the Caddy-saurous. You know, that sea monster you were telling us about the other day."

"Ah yes. The Cadborosaurus Willsi lives in Caboro Bay." Peter draped an arm over Walter's shoulders and started into a description of the CADDY from BC. "OH yes! Caddy is his nickname. But it has nothing to do with golf. It's named after the BC coastal bay where it was spotted. It's a long, serpent like beast with flippers, hair on the neck, and a camel's head. Although I haven't seen it, Caddy has been seen less than 100 times in the last 60 years. Unlike sightings of the Loch Ness monster and Ogopogo, the descriptions remain consistent and precise."

Peter is an amateur collector of sea monster stories like the Loch Ness monster, the Ogopogo from Lake Okanagan and this new one that he went out to British Columbia to see. His head turned side to side, examining the length of the pond and declared, "They say it can be 40 to 70 feet long in length. Not to worry, Michael, I doubt it will fit in this pond. They say it eats only seaweed and algae but it ate a duck once."

"Hey, Mikey, are you a decoy? A duck decoy? Are you on a mission to find the Caddy-monster?" George laughed like a hyena.

"You think because you're in there, none of us will hit into the pond?" Dr. Neville Decorte asked carefully. "Power of suggestion is very strong, Mikey. You draw the eye and someone might hit you. I suggest you drag yourself out of there."

"I heard you found a job, but I didn't know it was in show business," George Campbell said. "You're doing a pretty good acting job, Mikey. Is your new job at Marine World and you're practising to be the whale?"

"All the world is a stage, George. I saw you dancing and singing up on the tee."

"You kill me, Mikey," Walter said. "I never know what you'll do next."

"Life is full of surprises." Dr. Neville Decorte added, "How you manage the challenges builds character."

"What doesn't kill you, makes you stronger. That's an old Iroquois Indian proverb." George claimed aboriginal rights to that idea.

"Years ago, we psychiatrists used to prescribe hydrotherapy," Dr. Decorte said. "We'd tightly wrap the patient in sheets and let him sit in a tub of water until he calmed down. Now it is called time-out, counting to ten."

"Years ago they used to do lobotomies, too," I said.

George pointed up at the tee. "If we don't get a move on, they'll be doing lobotomies on us."

"You're the tenth group to come through here, doc. Any chance I can get out now?"

"Leave him in. It'll serve him right." Peter Mullen stared at me then sprouted a grin, followed by a snake-like tongue sticking out between his fat lips.

"Peter, I'm not the one who needs to control his temper."

"Temper, temper, Michael." The doc rubbed his chin, eyed the bulrushes, the edge of the pond, the distance from where he stood to my head. "Have you got a plan, Mikey? How are you going to get out of this mess?" Dr. Neville asked with a tone of voice as if I was a patient on his therapy couch.

"I'm working on it, Doc. Any advice will be gratefully appreciated."

"Come on, Doc. Like you tell your patients, they have to find their own solutions." George draped his arm around Dr. Decorte's shoulders and pulled him away. Dr. Decorte's solemn nod confirmed that I am on my own in this mess.

"So, Mikey, are you the designated decoy?"

"No, Peter. I'm the designated drunk."

"You mean the designated dunk. The fall guy. Ha!" Peter hurried to the green.

The local cops know the golfers at this course are heavy drinkers, especially after a major tournament. On a tournament day, the cops in a cruiser sit just down the road from the entrance. The guys have been stopped so often that they finally came up with a way to thwart the cops. As a cop watches, a golfer staggers out of the clubhouse, wobbles his walk, bumps into parked cars, and fumbles with his keys, nearly falling over trying to pick up his keys. Other members come out and get in their cars. The drunk continues to stagger around the parking lot, waves and yells at his buddies as they drive away. Finally the drunk is the last one in the parking lot and gets in his car and cruises toward the entrance of the club. The cop stops him and administers a breathalyser test that comes up totally clear of any alcohol content. The cop tests again, and baffled by the clear reading, finally asks the drunk.

The drunk says, "Damn well better be clear. I'm the designated drunk for tonight."

I've been the designated drunk on more than one occasion. Seriously drunk.

When my boss was arrested for theft and misappropriating funds, I almost told him I thought he was the designated decoy. His bosses should have been arrested, too. But as the cops locked handcuffs on him, he asked me to go and sit with his wife until he could get through the laying of charges, and I was to tell her he'd be home for dinner. I liked his wife. She was a good person. Not only did I know he was part of the problem and I could have been a witness for the prosecution, but he wanted me to keep his wife calm.

Maybe I was the designated dunk.

"Hey, Mikey," Walter called to me from the end of the pond nearer to the 18th tee. He had an unlit cigar in his hand and reminded me of Winston Churchill not only because he looks like Sir Winston, but also he's decided that just then is an elegant time to quote the man. "Mikey, you know what success is? Success is the ability to go from one failure to another with no loss of enthusiasm. Keep your chin up, kiddo."

Chapter 12

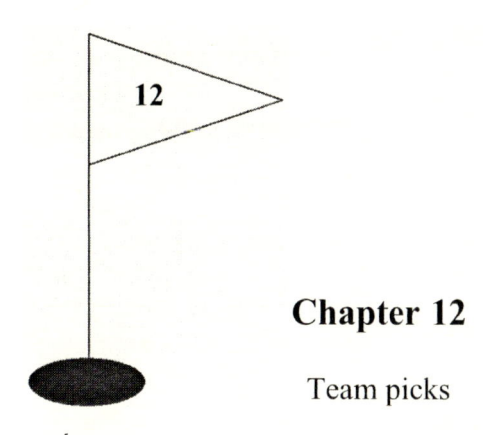

Team picks

It seems to me that Winston Churchill also said something about the types that see difficulty in every opportunity and those who see opportunity in every difficulty. I could see that I am definitely in a difficult situation. I haven't exactly looked for the opportunity, but I think analysing the foursomes coming off the 17th tee, trying to figure out who exactly could bring about the solution was a good start. One of the biggest parts of finding the solution is defining the problem.

The problem definitely was that I am stuck in the pond.

That done; now I know from all the courses I've taken that the next step is…

Nuts! This hydrotherapy is messing with my memory. Maybe I will get therapy, after I find a job, when I can afford it.

When I was living on employment insurance benefits I'd been through the free courses, paid for by Human Resources Development Canada. The contract counsellors talked about researching companies, networking, collecting and handing out business cards, write and re-write the resume, align the resumé to the company and job you're seeking, practice interview techniques, rehearse what you would say. Put a little spin on why you were laid off.

In truth, I was never actually fired. I was laid off during the restructuring, downsizing, re-engineering cycles of business. Like bookends, the recessions of the early nineties and the late nineties bordered a prosperous era. But this is early in the new century and the dot com failures, the airplanes dive bombing the World Trade Centre towers in New York, then the worldwide SARs virus, have all changed the economic territory and who knows how any employer is thinking. I heard some companies are not even opening their doors for drop-in job seekers, afraid that some SARs infected person would contaminate the front lobby.

Hunting down a job was akin to, well… hunting and fishing.

I researched companies as if mapping out an expedition into deepest, darkest Africa. One time when I was unemployed, I dug deeply into ENRON. And wow, things looked really promising for that company. Talk about spin.

I made a series of enquiries into a software company in the Ottawa area, and even convinced my wife that a move to Ottawa might be good for us. Just when I thought I might get an interview, my wife dropped a newspaper bomb on the kitchen table. The boss in Ottawa was being investigated by the Ontario Securities Commission. I practically wept.

My wife said, "Now you know why I'm so upset about Martha Stewart."

"Honey, what Martha Stewart does is not rocket science."

"Speaking of that industry, did you see that Trans Altagear is shutting down? Laying off twenty percent of their staff. Didn't you apply to them?"

"There goes that opportunity," I groaned.

Even when a company drops a line, with a baited hook, tugs to jiggle the lure, and then when the lure looks too good to be true and the sucker bites, the bigger, supposedly better pond may not be all it's hyped to be.

A very professional friend of mine was lured away from his lucrative sales job to be the sales manager at a fairly new company. The owner-slash-president and CFO said they needed his professionalism and wanted him to bring a new image to their company. As it turned out the president had a mouth full of words that even my father would have been ashamed of using.

The CFO and president didn't know how to turn up to appointments on time, if they turned up at all. They refused to pay my friend's business expenses and then one day, just shut him out, kept his list of contacts that he'd built up over years of professional conduct at other companies, and now my friend may have to sue his former employer to get his commissions, his expenses and his contact list out of the office he occupied for six months. Researching a company is a good plan, but you never know until you actually get inside that the company is all they proclaim to be or if the story is just camouflage.

I seriously want to work for a company that not only spouts a viable mission statement but actually lives up to the spin, has impeccable ethics, treats the employees fairly and is financially viable. I don't tell lies on my resumé but after months of hunting for the elusive beast, I was beginning to admire those who did lie and secured upper management positions. I admired the bravery, the chutzpah, the way they could sleep at night and yet rip off employees, pay less than minimum wages, ask that the staff take pay cuts, lose money for a company and stock holders and still take home a six million dollar bonus payment. After months of searching and holding out for the job that paid a decent wage, at a company that behaves with ethics, and finding nothing, I started to think that maybe I should be looking for a company that was hiding under the radar scope of the securities commission and maybe before that company collapsed I could walk away with a two million dollar bonus. Hell, I could manage a company a hell of a lot better than those guys and I wouldn't ask for as large a bonus.

My wife continued to ask about my job search and just to prove to her that I really was looking, I showed her the computer files about companies to which I had sent resumés. I told her about the interviews I had, the thank you letters I sent, the follow-up phone calls and emails I'd sent. I told her about the days I'd driven to Markham, spent an hour on the road to get to the interview, half an hour in the interview and then two hours to get home in 'rush' hour.

"And none of them thanked you for your time for your driving to the appointment, for your time and preparation researching the company?"

"Not a word. Nada."

"Well, that's rude. Don't they think your time is valuable? Do they think gasoline is free? Every trip you make costs money. A simple thank you for your time would be nice."

"Thank you."

"You're welcome."

"So now what?" she asked.

"I'll keep looking. Some days. Some days I'm just going to play golf."

"Oh. Are you any good at that?"

"Lately? No. My mind is… I sometimes I think I should be banging on doors, but executives are not hired by walking in the front door of a business. Assembly line, warehouse staff, even some clerks are hired that way but not executives. No, my golf game isn't improving. I can't focus. I'd like to work for a company with ethics, a company that values employees, reliability, and teamwork."

"Well," my wife rubbed my shoulder, "I'm on your team. Something will turn up."

"I'm going to hunt down the elusive beast. I'll find the hiding monster, take aim and shoot the sucker down."

"Go, team, go!" my wife cheered and marched out of my den, and I stared at the computer screen. The files were all listed by weekly dates, and each of those dated files held at least fifteen different companies to whom I had sent resumés. I no longer printed out the letters and resumés I sent out. If I did, the country would need a bigger budget for a reforestation.

I can't seem to find the team I wanted to work for, convince the interviewer that I will be a valuable member of the team. Hell, I can't even find a company that is polite enough to send me a thank-you-for-your-time note just for attending an interview. My wife might have been cheering me on, but she is the only one, at the moment.

Her blind compassion is inspiring, but my mood is sinking like the wheels of a golf cart in a pond. Her blind faith in me was moving, to say the least, but my depression frankly just sent me out to the sunshine of the golf course more and more often. At least out here no one asks me about my job. They all know I'm unemployed. Who but the unemployed or the retired play golf seven days a week?

The Human Resource and Development contract coaches all tell the unemployed to tell their friends and family that they are unemployed and looking and maybe one of their friends or family will know of an opening. Frankly, I'm not sure I want to work with any of my golfing friends. They probably don't want to work with me.

Golf was the only inspiring aspect. At least the sunshine of summer brightened my days.

I'm in a lousy mood, soaked up to my earlobes and recalling every unsuccessful interview. I'm sinking deeper and deeper.

Up on the tee, Alan Compton, and Frank Craig are lining up Bob Murtiss. Alan Compton and Bob Murtiss have been golfing partners for almost twenty years. They are always paired together in the same foursome. Visually they are as unlikely a pair as a beaver and a moose. Alan is a small man with a perpetual smile on his face and limitless energy, in constant motion. Bob is at least a foot taller and seldom moves, but he too has a permanent smile on his face. Bob always wears a white cowboy hat, dark glasses and his golf shirt and pants were always perfectly matched in colour, and immaculately put together. Even before Bob retired, rumour had it that his wife picked out his clothes.

Alan, on the other hand, would wear red and green plaid pants and a horizontally striped orange and blue shirt. He was like a walking test pattern. Just looking at Alan one could easily become dizzy. We all thought that Alan needed a wife to tell him how to dress.

Bob never seems to mind. Bob is legally blind.

Alan and Bob have been partners in golf and business for decades. They met on the golf course, played some rounds together and started talking business over a few drinks and the next thing they knew they were hooked together in the business world, played golf every Saturday and Sunday morning. Years before I joined the club, the two of them had a few arguments and split apart for awhile.

Then Bob's eyes started to fail and some of the members didn't want to play golf with him because he couldn't see where his drive landed, he's always lost and it slowed the game down for all the players. But then along came Alan, who took on the chore of guiding Bob around the course. Whatever argument they had that split them apart was totally forgotten or forgiven.

When Bob couldn't see at all, and medically declared blind, Alan still brought Bob out for a game of golf. They looked a little funny when Alan led Bob by the hand from the car to the pro shop. Someone must have commented about them looking like girlfriends because soon, they stopped holding hands and Bob would place his hand on Alan's shoulder whenever they had to cover any distance. On the course, they rode in a cart, with Alan steering, most of the time. Occasionally Bob would take over behind the wheel and Alan would give him directions. They are a noisy pair to play golf with.

In his youth Bob had a single digit handicap, hit a long ball, typically with a slice, but he could recover from any tricky place on the course. He was a scrambler.

After he lost his sight, Alan lines him up and his shots have straightened out. So as I watch them on the tee, with Bob facing the two guys, Alan facing the green, I can't actually hear Alan's advice but I know that he's saying, 'the flag is in the front right quadrant, tee blocks are five feet ahead of the yardage marker on the tee, breeze is…"

"I know what the breeze feels like up here, Alan," Bob would say. "I'm blind, not insensitive."

"The flag's not moving."

"Thank you," Bob would say. Then Alan would position Bob between the tee blocks, stand behind the ball, tell Bob to move his feet to line up appropriately, and Bob would take a swing. Alan would line up Bob's putts too, tell him the distance, the break and sometimes 'give' Bob long putts. Bob liked to hear the sound of a ball clunking into the bottom of a hole and sometimes the guys would just manoeuvre his still moving but missed putt ball into the hole, so Bob could hear that sound of completion and his playing partners would watch him grin.

Bob has risen to a 10 handicap. Alan's handicap has dropped, probably from giving Bob so much advice about Bob's alignment that he's improved his own faults. Sometimes Alan won't tell Bob his shot is in the sand and sometimes Alan kicks Bob's ball away from a tree. New comers to the club don't much like Alan fixing Bob's shots, but Alan makes sure Bob doesn't win any tournaments if he had cheated in Bob's favour that day. I'm pretty sure Bob knows that Alan kicks a ball away from a tree, picks Bob's ball out of a sand trap, fixes up his ball in the rough and gives Bob a good lie. Bob is a good guy and Alan is terrific for bringing Bob out to the course and nursemaid him through eighteen holes of golf. Alan is a much nicer guy because of it. Bob is too.

Apparently, they had been tough competitors in business and teaming up has been the best thing that they could ever have done. On the golf course they are probably the best two man better ball team. They may have argued as business partners, but once Bob lost his sight he believed and trusted Alan above all others. And both men have mellowed because of it.

If anyone would rescue me, I thought that Bob would, but somehow I have to let him know I'm stuck in the pond. I couldn't just whisper like I did to Al Kazan, whose religious convictions in response to my whispering from the bulrushes nearly gave him a heart attack. I have to convince Alan Compton to convince Bob that I'm stuck in the pond. Somehow I have to recruit Alan and Frank to convince Bob that I really am mired in muck. Bob wouldn't leave me there. Bob is a nice guy. A forgiving man.

I had to draw Alan's attention without spooking Bob.

Frank Craig, on the other hand, isn't too fond of me. And since he's the third player in the group, I probably have a better chance of drawing Frank over to talk to me without Bob hearing my waterlogged voice mysteriously coming up from the pond.

So I couldn't just talk to Frank from the pond because Bob's hearing is pretty good and he might sense direction by sound. He'll know I'm talking from the surface of the pond. Someone once joked that he's like a bat, with radar capabilities and because of that some of us called him 'Batman.' When he heard the nickname, Bob grinned and laughed. Apparently, Batman comic books are his favourite.

As they lined up Bob to make his shot from the cliff top tee, I tried to focus on what I would do and say to enlist their help. I could shake my body to create ripples and draw Alan's gaze. He'll be curious and come over to the edge of the pond, but he'll have Bob on the cart with him. Frank will be walking and slower coming down the hill than the two on the cart. Since all three of these guys hit the green probably ninety percent of the time they are on the 17th tee, the odds are that none of them will drop a shot in the pond.

I had to do something to mess up Frank's tee shot and hope he'd flop shot it into my watery situation, then have to drop a ball on the tee side of the pond.

From my perspective Bob's tee shot looked really good, high flyer and straight off the tee, over my head and I could hear it thud on to the green behind me. Then Alan was on the tee and he had a sweet swing. His shot travelled a similar line to Bob's. Next up is Frank Craig and he has a routine that drove some players nuts.

When I played with Frank, being a numbers guy, I tend to count the number of times he re-grips his club and waggles. One time I counted eighteen re-grips. Some of the guys would start snoring just to give him the hint that he has to play faster. Some guys call him "Sergio" because Sergio Garcia had the same re-grip, re-grip, re-grip style. I've heard a rumour that Frank is down to under ten re-grips before he actually starts his back swing. I wanted to screech like an owl right in the middle of his back swing, screw up his shot and hopefully he'd drop the shot into the pond and then see me.

In the back of my mind I counted his waggles and re-grips, trying to judge when to screech but right at the front of my brain the list of things that I've done to Frank came out like a storm warning. When he got to twelve re-grips and waggles, I had a list of twelve ways I've pissed off Frank. The biggest loomed like the ice storm in Quebec that had shut down the province for at least a week. And like one of those Quebec hydroelectric towers, I froze and my decision collapsed.

I can't think of one thing that I've done to redeem my sorry soul in Frank's eyes. He's probably still mad at me for romancing Melanie and ruining any chances he had with her. In his mind that was the twelfth and last straw that ruined any chance of us ever playing in the same foursome again, let alone him rescuing my waterlogged body.

My only recourse was to call out to Alan Compton and hope the man with the kind heart toward his blind partner will yank me out of the pond.

The cart was halfway down the hill.

"HEY, ALAN!" I yelled. "BOB! It's me. Michael Blaine."

The riding cart slowed. I yelled again. "ALAN. Over here! In the pond!"

The cart came to the tee side edge of the pond and Alan stared at me. Bob's face was turned toward Alan's. His mouth moved but I can't hear him. Alan's mouth is moving too.

"Listen, Alan, Bob..." One should always include Bob in the conversation. "I could use some help getting out of here."

"What are you doing in the pond?" Alan left the cart and stood at the side of the pond. Then Bob climbed out and started walking toward the pond.

"NO! Bob! Whoa. Stop!" I bellowed.

Just as Bob's foot hovered over the water, Alan grabbed his blind partner and pulled him back to dry land.

"Jesus, Bob! You scared me," I said.

"I thought we were at the green. Where are we?" Bob aimed his face toward Alan.

"Mikey Blaine is in the pond," Alan said.

"What's he doing in the pond?"

"Not much."

Frank joined them by then. The man shook his head, then smiled. "I guess you didn't hear the rumours."

"What rumours?" I asked.

Frank giggled. "You ought to be more careful about picking your partners. You're lucky I wasn't in your foursome, Mikey."

I didn't like the look on Frank's face.

"Why is Mikey in the pond? What's he doing in the pond? Will someone please tell me?" Bob asked as Alan tried to steer him back into the cart.

"BOB! Can you help me out?" I yelled again.

Bob turned and faced my bellows. "I'm blind, Mikey. Not deaf!"

"Sorry, Bob."

"Being blind I couldn't even throw a lasso over to you." Bob started toward the edge of the pond again. Alan was at the back of the cart. "Why is Michael in the pond?" Bob faced where he thought Frank was.

"He's just lucky. If it'd been me, I'd have thrown him in head first." Frank called from the left end of the pond as he walked toward the green.

"You never were a nice man, Frank," Bob said and aimed his face toward me.

If I didn't know he is blind I could have sworn he could see me.

"He never was," Bob whispered in my direction.

"Mikey, I don't have a rope to throw at you," Alan called from behind Bob.

"My hands are tied, Alan," I said. "I couldn't catch it."

"Come on, you guys. Let's finish this game," Frank pleaded from the green.

Bob turned his head, then his body.

"Come on, Bob. We'll have to figure this out, later," Alan said.

"HURRY UP!" Frank yelled.

Bob turned again. Then his foot slipped and he went down, and slid like a snake into the water. My shoulders yanked up as if I could hold out my arms and catch him. Alan yelled. Frank came running, feet thudding around the pond.

For a moment the sun shone on his face. Bob stared at me as he lounged back against the edge of the pond. Then like a goose trying to take flight his arms flapped, grabbed and groped and I stood there helplessly watching as Frank and Alan pulled, turned him and helped Bob out of the water. Alan patted small golf towels at Bob's lower wet half. He pushed away Alan's hands and slapped at his wet pants. "You shouldn't have yelled at me, Frank," Bob said as he staggered a bit, then found the cart and sat. The look on his face was like a surprised mutt.

The cart started to move away.

Bob yelled and waved a golf towel as the cart headed toward the green. "We'll be back! Keep the faith, Mikey!"

All I could think of was to wonder if the blind know how to swim. But as Bob said, he's blind not deaf. I don't know if he was trying to walk into the pond and rescue me or accidentally slipped. Life is full of hazard. For a blind man the hazards must seem endless. With the right teammate even Bob could manage.

I'm thankful that he's out of the pond and had faith that he would be back, with a team, to pull me out.

Chapter 13

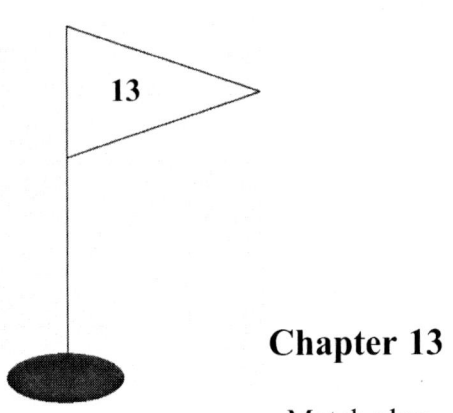

Match play
Golf and marriage go together like a sailboat and anchor

Trusting that Bob and Alan will be back in a short while, I stopped worrying about my rescue and let my mind venture off to the list of hazards Bob, or any golfer for that matter, can face on the golf course.

The pro says a sandtrap is the friendliest of all hazards. At least you can find the ball. If the ball lands in a sand trap, you haven't lost the ball and a stroke and distance as you will if you hit a shot out-of-bounds. If the ball lands inside the hazard stakes, around a pond, there are rules about how to hit the ball. Don't touch the ground or a penalty stroke will be added to your score. If the ball is perched on granules of sand, it's not at the bottom of a pond, which results in a lost ball, and a stroke.

Some golfers are so good at playing out of the sand they'd rather be in a sandtrap than in the long rough beside the green. They will aim for the bunker because they know how to control the shot to get out. It's an easier shot to control than trying to hit out of the fescue.

Fescue is that extra long grass beyond the long grass called rough and a lot of us macho types try to slash our way out of the weeds of fescue and plan to move the ball forward. I've tried this a few times but more often than not I manage to help the ball slide deeper and deeper into the tangled web of the weeds. I know some golfers who don't bother to look for a ball in the fescue, but take an unplayable lie, go back along the line of flight and make a shot from there.

There are definite rules for playing from hazards. Just about every golf course scorecard lists the local rules for hazards. If your ball lands in a flowerbed you usually get a free lift. If your ball hits a fence and drops you may get a free lift or have to hit from behind a fence and pitch a shot straight out to the fairway. Check the course score card for the local rules.

I'm now thinking I should have asked my wife for the definitive descriptions and rules for playing around her hazards. I wish there were red stakes around her danger zones. I wish that her sinister and beguiling moods were as easy to get out of as sandtraps. I've tried flashing my way out of arguments with my wife, but the more my mouth bursts forth with fescue fibs, the deeper my predicament becomes. I learned over the years that the best action is to follow the unplayable rule right away and move forward. Believe me, the more you hack at the lies and falsehoods, the deeper the do-do you'll be in.

As it is, I've been living in a bunker, like a Cold War underground bunker, with no hope of seeing the light of day once the nuclear reaction of my wife's anger reverberates through the house.

If wives came packaged with score cards that listed the local attributes of an immovable object, we husbands wouldn't be in such deep fescue so often. We could just spout the rule, take a free lift and move on.

Bill Clement and his wife Monica, Earl Harris and his wife MaryAnn are on the tee. I'm overjoyed to see these guys.

One July day, I had the pleasure of playing a round of golf with Earl Harris. As we stood on the tee of the par-three seventh hole, waiting for the group ahead of us to clear the green, Earl asked if my wife played golf.

"No she doesn't, Earl. Why?"

"My wife is a beginner. Know how I knew when she was hooked to the game? One Friday night we played as partners in the mixed couples nine-hole tournament. MaryAnn had been working hard at learning the game and her drive that night on this, the seventh hole, landed on the green. It was a first. She was ecstatic. That night we made love like never before. As we laid exhausted, side by side, she sighed. I was feeling seriously proud of the success of our event. My ego was fair to bursting with accomplishment."

"Okay."

Earl went on, "As I said, I learned that night, she was hooked on the game. There we were on the bed, recovering nicely. She sighed again, snuggled up close, gazed into my eyes, with sparkles in her eyes and said, 'Did you see my shot on the seventh hole?'"

"So this hole has fond memories for you?" I asked.

"Oh, yeah. So, I think you should teach your wife to play golf. She'll be able to play with you in your retirement years, kind of like a built-in golfing partner. My wife didn't like being alone Saturdays and Sundays. She didn't like being a golf widow. She couldn't understand the fascination of the game so she joined up. That old saying, if you can't beat 'em, join 'em. And I kind of like it. Now when we go on holidays we both take our golf clubs."

The day I moved out Sharon said, "Since I'm already a golf widow I might as well live alone, like a real widow."

Earl and his wife are a really nice couple. That day on the seventh tee, after hearing his story, I didn't have the heart to tell Earl that my wife and I had split up.

But he probably knows by now.

Playing with Earl and his wife are Bill Clement and his wife. Billy Clement used to look a lot like Bill Clinton, the ex-president of the US of A and even a little more unusual is that Monica Clement looks something like Bill Clinton's infamous secret partner. One Halloween Bill and Monica Clement came to the golf club's last social event and final dance of the season, dressed like that other notorious pair.

Bill and Monica Clement are good people. We're friends. Bill would get me out of this pond just like I protected him in Myrtle Beach.

Bill Clement and his wife Monica had been good friends of mine and my wife's, but at this moment I'm hoping Bill remembers how I, along with some other guys, rescued his life on one of our trips to Myrtle Beach. I'll never forget the year eight of us guys rented a van, and while six of us drove down to South Carolina, Bill and Ron flew down on a cheap flight out of Buffalo two days later and we planned to pick them up at the airport.

All six of us went to the Myrtle Beach airport to meet Bill and Ron. We left Paul with the van to guard the equipment while five of us ventured into the airport and marched through like a vanguard of new recruits. It was the day we had decided to wear our black matching golf shirts and black pants as if we were some sort of team. We all sported dark sunglasses and tried to look like heroes from *Men in Black*.

Our marching antics, like a mercenary team on a mission drew, some surprised looks but also parted the crowd, like Moses parted the Dead Sea. Just ahead of us were a half dozen security guards all hurrying along the same route we took. We could hear the buzz of anticipation as we approached the arrival gate. A couple of dozen people hung around, whispering and staring at the door the passengers would come through.

I asked one of the onlookers what was going on and she looked around, leaned in close and whispered, "Bill Clinton is on the plane."

"This one? This flight from Buffalo?" I asked.

She nodded.

As quietly as I could I told the guys, who grinned.

"You mean Billy C? Our Billy C," Jeff whispered.

I nodded. "Remember? We thought Billy looked like him when he and Monica got married. Last year. You know who Monica looks like?"

"Bill didn't bring Monica, did he? This is a guys golfing week," one of them groaned.

"The ex-President is on the plane from Buffalo?" Mark asked in a clear whisper. He winked at me and pulled out his retired cop badge wallet. With that he and I went to the front of the line and showed it to the rent-a-cop security troops who backed off and allowed us to be the first to greet the ex-president of the United States.

Bill Clement and Ron came off the plane first, saw us, and waved. Mark and I rushed into the corridor, with our three counterparts guarding the doorway, holding back the crowd. We surrounded Billy, whispered to him that he had to act like Billy Clinton.

"I know. The stewardess thought I was Mr. C." Billy Clement grinned. "Free drinks all the way here, first class seats." Billy Clement had played this act before so he did the grin, the wave, and then we rushed him through the participating observers. We kept Billy hemmed in as we retrieved his luggage and golf bag. We caused quite a stir but escaped quickly from the airport.

In the van, we all had a good laugh about the incident.

And then when we checked in for our game of golf, the pro at the golf course stared at Bill like he's the real Bill. The pro even started to ask me, "Is that Bill—"

I interrupted with a shush! And whispered, "He's trying to keep a low profile."

Our group got free green fees at that club. And at dinner that night the waitress asked if 'that was President—' Well, of course, I interrupted her too. We tipped her well for keeping the secret and we managed to get a free meal. Four couples stopped by our table to tell Mr. Clinton what an honour it was to meet him.

Bill's favourite phrase that week was a meek grin and 'no comment' comment.

We kept up the gambit for as long as we could, but then on our third day, there was a problem. A citizen took real offense at what Mr. Clinton had done to Hillary and tried to defend Hillary's honour. An altercation ensued and we had a hell of a time explaining to the local cops that Bill Clement was definitely not The Mr. Clinton.

Then the local cops wanted to arrest him for impersonating the ex-president and we all had to vouch for our buddy Bill Clement. We spent about three hours at the cop shop where we promised, as a condition of parole, that we would make an early departure from Myrtle Beach. We figured the safest way to get Bill home was if we all went back in the van.

Back in Canada I suggested that the guys drop me and Bill at my house and I would drive him home from there. I thought Bill might need a collaborating witness when he had to explain to Monica that the black eye he sported happened while defending Hillary.

Monica wanted to know who Hillary was.

So now, as I watch the four of them, Earl and his wife, the nicest couple at the club, and Bill and Monica Clement, one of the funniest couples at the club, I could just about taste the brandy I'm going to order as my reward for surviving captivity in the pond. I was pretty sure I'd get an executive parole, clemency. I couldn't have prayed for a better foursome to drag me out of the pond. This foursome is a match made in heaven.

As they dragged their golf pull-carts down the tarmac path I felt warmer already. I put on my best smile and called out, "Hey, Mr. Clinton? Monica! Come over here. Mr. President, I could use an executive order. A parole?"

They walked over to the edge of the pond and the four of them stood there looking at me. Silent, like mourners.

"It's me. Michael Blaine. How about an executive decision? A pardon? Bill, remember Myrtle Beach? The week everyone thought you were the ex-president. Remember? Come on, Bill, pull me out?"

Monica was the first one to speak. "When hell freezes over." She marched away. Her voice echoed with something my wife will probably say.

Bill watched her, looked at me, looked at Earl who watched MaryAnn who had followed Monica toward the green.

"Earl? Bill?" I asked again.

"EARL!" Mrs. Harris yelled.

Earl followed her.

"Come on, Bill!" Monica yelled. "You have a birdie putt. I've got money riding on this putt. We can win the match."

Bill rocked on his heels. Rose up on his toes and eyed the green. He settled back down. Eyeing me with those sad Bill Clinton eyes, he leaned in and whispered, "Jesus, Mikey. My wife and yours are still friends."

"Bill?" I begged. "Come on, Bill. Give me a pardon. Help me out of here."

He hesitated and I thought for a flashing second that I'm going to be rescued, pardoned by our very own 'Bill Clinton.'

"Bill! Come on. Let's finish off this match!" Monica called from beyond the bulrushes, from behind me, from the green.

I had to draw Bill's attention again, so I asked, "Bill, make a presidential decision, Bill. Please? A presidential statement—"

"No comment." Bill walked away.

Boy, did I pick the wrong group. I'd forgotten how close Monica and my wife are and that Monica would take sides with her. And I guess just like Bill Clinton, Bill Clement had to say the right thing. Unfortunately, it isn't in my favour. I'm Billy Clement's Monica Lewinsky.

Chapter 14

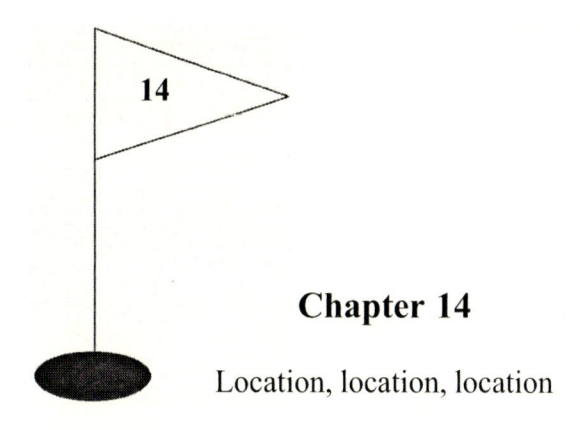

Location, location, location

Billy Clement became tired of being pointed out as a clone of Bill Clinton, so he changed his hairstyle, lost some weight, talked Monica into dyeing her hair. They were in full-speed-ahead mode to change their looks. Of course when Bill and Hillary Clinton had to move out of the White House, they had to change a few things. Location for one, lifestyle and the political protocol. Even in golf, changing courses isn't a bad idea.

A couple of years ago our course went through some major renovation and through reciprocal agreements with other golf clubs, we had privileges to play at those other courses. Looking back on that summer, it really was fun.

My course, CrossCreek, except for the 16th and 17th, is a fairly flat course. It's a par seventy-two, with a slope rating of one hundred and fifteen which most of us think is underrated. CrossCreek has its challenges, especially if the wind is blowing out of the east. As anyone who lives in Ontario knows, the worst storms come from the east. We got Hurricane Isabel from the southeast but she, much like my girlfriend Melanie, turned out to be a bit of a dud.

If the wind blows across our fairways and comes from the east, it means a golfer on the 7th, 8th, 12th, 15th and 17th holes is hitting dead into the wind. High ball hitters might hit a huge shot but up there in the sky the ball acts like it hit a wall and stops dead in its tracks and drops like a stone. On the 16th an east wind is helpful to hookers whose balls fly even farther left and practically land on the green of the par-4 hole. If a player hits a slice, the wind might just keep the ball up on the plateau and out of the creek. On the 17th, par-three hole, with an east wind, you have to power your shot over the pond and onto the landing bailout area. On the other holes of the CrossCreek course, creeks are a bit of a hazard, but we've played the course so often, we know the lay of the land so well, we can practically dial-in our scores.

At the other courses that we played that summer two years ago, golfers had to think about the lay of the land, think about distance, be aware of the hazards, and strategize before every shot. So the different courses, in the long run, made us all better golfers. Playing at other courses, like public courses, gave me a whole new set of losers—ah, I mean, players to challenge.

I had a whole new audience to entertain, bets to try, match play to win, and a whole new set of pockets to pick. All I had to do was call the pro shop and get a tee time, sign up as a single and then watch my three playing partners as they fidget on the first tee, trying to calm first tee jitters, and bragging about their handicaps which we couldn't check because there was no computer in which to enter and to track our scores. All they had to go on about my handicap was my say so. And of course that's all I had to go on about theirs. I must admit watching these strangers before they teed off, I honed my skills of analysing players. Unless I was really off my game, I could make money hustling a few bucks from strangers.

There are obvious clues about a player's capability. Some golfers are better than others at hiding his first tee jitters. Some are great braggers, great actors. But the best way to tell an Oscar winning bragger is look at his equipment. While I'm standing at the first tee, listening to the excuses for the day, it's the easiest thing to do. I check the opponents' equipment.

First up, I check out his attire. Is he wearing the latest Tiger Woods neckline? Is he wearing worn down soft spikes in his FootJoy golf shoes? Do the pockets of his pants have wear marks at the pockets? All signs of a long time player, but he's at a public course, right?

Then I do a visible check of his golf bag. Is it a carry bag like a Sun Mountain? Is it a big, fat leather tour bag? Is it a brand name bag, or is it emblazoned with a product logo like, say, Coors Light? Is it old and stuffed pockets are bulging, or is it clean and new?

Next, I watch how he looks for a ball to play. Does he open a new three ball sleeve of Titliest, Staff or MaxFli balls? Does he dig in his bag and check for marks and wear spots on his old ball? Does he actually check to see if the ball is 'out of round'? All of these are clues to his passion for the game.

Then, I have a look at the clubs in his bag. No matter what kind they are, I verbalise my admiration. He owns them, he's proud of them. I never insult a man's car or his sport. Now as I'm admiring his clubs, I count the number of wedges in his bag. The more wedges he has the better the player. At this point, I don't worry too much about his putter. Because putting is such a finesse part of the game, no one can tell by the shape, brand, or colour of a putter, if he's any good with it. Hopefully, I've seen him on the putting green and know what he can and can not do.

So now that I've checked out his attire and his equipment, I listen carefully to his excuses. "I didn't have time to practice." "I was at a party last night and boy, am I hung over." "These are my old shoes." "My shoulder hurts." "These are my new shoes." Yeah, right, and the dog ate my homework.

The ones I'm wary of are the guys wearing the comfortable golf shirt, the well-fitted golf shoes, clean sharp soft spikes, and half a dozen wedges in his bag, and from his bag he pulls out a brand new sleeve of balls and doesn't say a word about his excuses. The quiet ones are the dangerous ones. Their successes will sneak up on you.

If a player can actually aim, hit and land his shot on the best strategic spot on the fairway, like a billiards player always plans where he will 'leave' his cue ball, then I know he's a damn good player.

So, "location, location, location" doesn't just apply to real estate.

Playing that summer at some other courses increased my net worth.

But then, as it turned out, my wife thought it was time to relocate our marriage. I relocated to an apartment with just a couple of pieces of furniture from the rec room. So it was a good thing I was pocketing some cash at golf because now I had to pay my own rent, food, and expenses as well as pay half the costs of the house she lived in.

She said my relocation was because we had too many arguments on Friday nights. Obviously she didn't understand that I had to play stellar golf the next day and arguing on Friday nights was my anger management technique.

Moving out of the house put a stop to the Friday night arguments with my wife. But then, as I've now discovered, my living alone is a lot like living in a swamp. When I can't find my favourite lucky golf shirt, I figure the cockroaches in that building have taken it for their nest. When I saw one of the illegal dogs in the building marching around with my sport sock in his mouth, I know I've forgotten to collect my laundry from the communal basement laundromat. There was no point trying to pull the sock from the mutt. He has bigger teeth than I do. Relocating out of my wife's domain wasn't such a good idea. But nothing else seemed to work.

When all else fails, relocate. Get out while the getting out is good. There has to be ways to clue into when it's time to pack up your tent and leave town. I aligned that thought to knowing when my job was about to end. I became so good at it, I predicted when more layoffs were about to happen. I recognized that when my boss didn't talk to me, didn't look me in the eye, that I've done something wrong or I'm on the layoff list. When I caught someone else working on projects that I thought were coming my way, a pink slip was also headed my way. I really clued in when my benefits were cut off, and I found out my wife changed the front door lock, the girlfriend didn't return my calls. And I knew the bottom of the barrel was fast approaching that morning I staggered around the apartment trying to fathom what to do next but was too drunk to remember where I worked, if I worked.

But there is nothing so uplifting as a new job. Those first days in a new office are titillating. My nerves practically explode with optimism and energy. My ego sits on top of my head like a Jesper

Parnevik baseball cap and one word is written on the upturned brim: HIRED!

My fingers slide over my name on the office door, stroke the desk. My hands grip the arms of my chair, caressed the computer keyboard and I whisper, 'mine.' All those months of hunting for a job have finally paid off. When I received my first pay cheque I kissed the pay deposit notification slip as if I'd just received my annual membership card to the golf club of my choice.

Out at the golf club I wanted to hand out my brand spanking new business card as if it was the gilt edged announcement to a very exclusive club. But there is an unwritten rule that we don't talk about business on the golf course. And adults are not supposed to leap and dance for joy like Snoopy the dog. But I have a job, and I can afford to pay the annual green fee dues and place a bet or two. I danced better than Snoopy.

My ego was restored, renewed and I was ready to relax and play ball.

I bought new golf clubs, stocked up on the newest long distance golf balls, sported my new company's golf shirt and logo baseball cap. I was ready, should anyone ask me, to describe my new job, my new company and I smiled with my head held high. I could relax and play some really decent golf because underneath I'm no longer worried about the economy. What me worry? I have a job. A job! And with my skills I'm destined to clean up on the golf course, too.

I didn't recognize the fourth member of the group on the 17th tee but I identify Joey Zamora, Danny Smart, and Tim Bond. All three of them are salesmen. Joe sold Chryslers. Danny is a commercial real estate agent and Tim is an investment advisor. I'm not sure if anyone has ever said to their faces, that they are our local three stooges, like Larry, Curly, and Moe. The three salesmen hang out together. There were times the rest of us left the bar to get away from these guys, because these guys tried to sell swampland in Florida or an acre of moon land. If any one of this foursome might have an iota of sympathy for me, it may well be the stranger, but as they came down the path, I still can't recognize the fourth member of the group.

Danny came over to the pond, removed his baseball cap and rubbed his baldhead. "Hey, Mikey. You look really comfortable in there. I've got some swampland in Florida you'd like," the real estate agent said.

"All you have to do is drain the swamp." Joey chuckled.

"Just like always, it looks like you're all wet." Tim grinned as he took his position beside Joey.

"What are you doing in there, Mikey? A little contact fishing?" Joey asked.

"I didn't know fishing was a contact sport?" Danny peered at Joey.

"Are you wrestling the gold fish into submission?" Tim nudged Joey's arm.

"Until today, I didn't know golf was a contact sport," I said, hoping to stop their comedy routine. "Joey, I don't suppose you drove a Jeep to the course today. Could you go and get it, and a rope, and drag me out of here?"

"I bet the guys changed the rules again and didn't tell all of us. Is this part of a triathlon, Mikey? Golf, run, and swim?" Danny asked. "Nobody ever tells us nuthing. Speaking of rules. Mikey, did you know the RCGA says you aren't allowed to put your hand in a water hazards to retrieve your balls?"

"Too late now, Danny," I said.

"Speaking of late, on that note, gotta run, Mikey." Joey turned on his heel and headed around the pond. The fourth player stared at me. He looked a little familiar.

Tim hitched up his pants. "Yep. Gotta run. I heard Al Kazan got a hole-in-one. Is that right, Mikey? Did you hear that? Did they tell you that? Might be the last hole-in-one of the season. We have to use up the hole-in-one fund. Maybe we'll all get more than one drink." Tim, no doubt, knew exactly how much is left in the hole-in-one fund.

"I heard that, Tim. And I could use a drink about now."

"Mikey, you are in the drink. Drink all you want." Tim laughed hysterically.

"Guys, guys. What we have here is a failure to communicate. I'd like to get out of here."

"Is that Michael Blaine? Is that the Michael Blaine who used to work at Cancom? I know you. You're the one." The fourth player turned and waved over at his host. "Joey! That's the accountant who wouldn't approve my expenses. Makes me do all my expenses twice. You're the guy who wouldn't approve my trip to Winnipeg. I know you." He pointed at me like a Supreme Court judge.

I recognized the fourth player now. Like a ghost from the wicked past, his gravel-edged voice is unmistakable. "Every time you did your expenses twice, Andy, I had to check them twice."

"But Jesus, Mikey, you'd think it was your money."

"It was my money. Your expenses weren't legitimate sales expenses, and ate into the company profits. Every employee got bonuses based on profits. Andy, I could have lost my job."

"You did lose your job." Andy laughed.

"I didn't lose my job because of screwing the books. If you hadn't tried to claim a month's worth of laundry on a two-night trip to Winnipeg… the first time, I wouldn't have had to check all of your expense reports. Do your laundry at home, Andy."

"What's a little money laundering? Eh, Mikey." Tim elbowed his salesman buddy.

"You could have lost your job, Andy. As it was, you just wasted my time. Hey, Andy, Andy, did you hear the one about the salesman who phoned Donna, the equipment scheduler? He greeted her, chit chatted about the weather, the local politics, ages of her kids, and generally blathered on. Donna asked, 'So, what can I do for you?'

"So the salesman said, 'Wait, Donna, I got a good joke for you?'

"'Okay. Tell me a joke,'" she says.

"The salesman began his joke. 'What's the definition of eternity?'

"You know what she said, Andy?"

Andy cocked his head and frowned. "No, Michael. What's the definition of eternity?"

"Talking to a salesman."

Andy glared at me, his jaw dropped. He opened and closed his mouth a couple of times and then his host, Tim, pulled Andy away from the pond and they left me in peace.

Unfortunately, they also left me in the pond. Just because I was in a dicey situation, up to my neck in water lilies, that doesn't mean I can't stand up for what is right. With that head-to-head battle won, hot to trot on the heels of that victory, I glared up to the tee for the next foursome.

Chapter 15

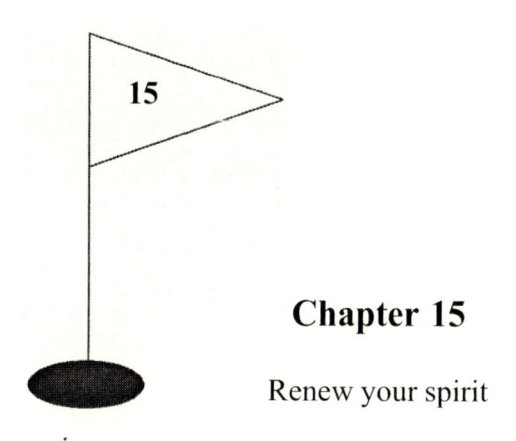

Renew your spirit

Four women!

The business ladies!

These are reasonable people. Women are sympathetic, nurturing, maternal, and somehow I would tug at their hearts to get them to yank me out of here. They are speed players, and already I can see the gathering group up on the 17th tee as the foursome behind this first group of ladies came off the 16th green.

Haven't I promoted the mixed tournaments, encouraged the guys to play golf with the women. I even had a huge argument with a group of guys that the ladies play faster than the guys. The fact that there are now two foursomes on the 17th tee is a testament to that fact.

The business ladies play an average round of golf in four hours or less. They explained it. "Things to do, places to go." Women golfers play fast because they have a long list of other things to accomplish on any given day of the week. Most of the women golfers I know take fewer than two practice swings. The men take an average of five practice swings. I have statistics on all of them.

The business ladies would drag me out of the pond. Women did more, accomplished more at all the companies I had ever worked for. They can multitask!

I'm surely going to be saved by the women.

Four ladies lined up at the edge of the pond facing me. Melanie is one of them. I'm not totally afraid of her. Our last private conversation didn't ended in the ditch. I had hopes we would still be friends. Beside her is Ruth, a tall, lanky single digit handicapper, and beside Ruth is Audrey, who always laughs when she hits a bad shot and then as if she has an extremely short-term memory always hits a good shot. She never lets bad shots ruin her game. Last but not least is Debbie, one of the smallest women at the club.

"He doesn't look like a frog," Ruth said.

"Trust me. If you kiss him, he doesn't turn into a prince," Melanie advised all within earshot.

"Caught coming up short again, Mikey?" Audrey asked.

"Tall is a state of mind," I shot back.

Their words came faster than an AK-47 on automatic firing.

"Still managing to keep your head above water?"

"Mikey! You're upside down. I thought she told you to go soak your head."

"That's an awful long cold shower, Mikey."

"And another thing…"

"Don't pout at us, Mikey. If you think we're going to yank your sorry ass out of there, think again!"

"That's the point. I am sorry!" I said clearly.

"Frost warning for tonight, Mikey. And it'll be a frosty Friday before any of us haul you out of there. Too bad tomorrow is Sunday."

"There's a swamp rat if I ever saw one."

"He doesn't need a swamp to be a rat."

"Come on, ladies. Take your best shot. Keep 'em coming. Don't stop now." As if my begging for more cheap shots stopped them, there was a sweet moment of silence. In the distance, like a war whoop, a dog's bark sounded. Kaida came loping down the path from the back shop and clubhouse. He barked twice more. Reared up like the Lone Ranger's faithful stallion and ran toward them.

While three of the women looked over their shoulders to watch the dog, Debbie leaned forward and asked, "There aren't any leeches in there, are there, Mikey?"

"Just one. Him!" Melanie shot back.

"Where's your nurturing heart? Where are the warm hearted business ladies I know and respect?"

"Why is that, Mikey?" Ruth asked. "Why do you respect us?"

Kaida arrived and nosed in between Ruth and Melanie and barked his arrival. Melanie's hand stroked the dog that looked up at her with pure affection. Stupid dog. He was supposed to bring reinforcements, but at the moment, from my vantage point, he sided with these verbally dangerous females.

"Why do I respect you? You are fast players. You follow the rules. You only give short gimmes. You're quick. You're fine human beings. I don't know why the guys don't like playing with you. I don't know why the guys don't like you playing from the men's tees."

My words recharged, reloaded their AK-47s and out shot a slew of verbal bullets.

"Because we beat them."

Kaida barked in agreement.

"From their tees."

"Because we catch them when they cheat."

"We beat them at their own game."

Kaida barked twice.

"And we don't cheat to do it." The three most vocal business ladies marched on over to the green. "Come on, Kaida." Kaida watched them go, glanced back at me, then at the ladies and started following them.

"Kaida, you traitor!" I bellowed out. Kaida barked, head in the air and pranced after the females.

Debbie McCall, one of the shyest, quietest lady golfers, watched them go, offered up a sympathetic shrug and a half wince. Debbie's voice was soft and warm, beckoning. "Mikey?"

"Yeah, Deb?"

"I got a tip for you."

I smiled my warmest brightest smile. "I'm listening."

"Your boat's got holes in it." She howled and slapped her knee then called out to the others on the green. "His boat's got holes in it! That's a good one, isn't it? Isn't that a good one?" Debbie hurried along the front of the pond toward the 18th tee.

"Yeah, well, you ladies always were lousy tippers!"

That bellow of mine was punctuated by a ball landing in the pond and I had to look up at the tee. It was Jeanne Clark. Our best woman golfer, ladies club champion five years in a row, and Ontario Amateur champion. And she was teeing it up again.

That one was a high flyer and landed inches from my right shoulder. "Hey! What did I ever do to you?"

One of her playing partners tossed another ball to her. It reminded me of a coach hitting baseballs to give the fielders some practice. Jeanne can be more accurate than the Blue Jays coach. Panic came at me as fast as her shots from the tee.

"Jeanne! I caddied for you at the…"

Plunk! A ball landed a foot in front of my face, splattered water at me as I finished the sentence.

"Amateur!" I yelled at the wrong moment. Even from the pond I can see that she's more determined to refine her aim. I didn't much like being used for target practice and thought she was being unreasonable.

"Jeanne? I always let you play from the men's tees." It's true. I hated it when she beat me from the yellows, the ladies tees, so when I played golf with her I insisted that she play from my tees. I hated it even more when she beat me from the longer tees, but I paid my debts. Hell, she's a low single digit handicapper. I'm a ten or fifteen.

That shot missed me by ten yards. Then she teed it up and used a different club. I heard the ball land on ground behind me and hope it's within birdie range on the green. Her mood improves as birdies fly into the cup.

The other three players with her all made good shots to the green. At least from my angle, with the line of flight over my head the shots look good to me.

None of them stopped to talk to me. I'm a little thankful of that. I wouldn't win any arguments with the business ladies. I don't win many against my wife and I don't have the guts to admit she's right.

Then I felt these little pinpricks at the back of my head. Turning my head as much as I can, I can't see them but I can see white tees floating around me. They're sniping at me, tossing tees from the green side of the pond. In seconds, floating tees surround me and as the things circle me, like a flotilla of miniature battle ships, and the points are all aimed at me.

I closed my eyes until I heard them cross the bridge to the eighteenth tee. Then I looked up at the sky and formed an image in my mind, of exactly what the 'Golf God' looks like.

I picture him as a smiling, blue-eyed Santa Claus. He has white hair and a neatly trimmed white beard, like cotton ball white clouds. He has a belly that laughs heartily whenever a golfer make a bad shot, and laughs twice as hard when the ball takes a bad bounce. His head would shake back and forth whenever a golfer overpowers a swing and yanks a shot. He'll giggle when the self-deceptors use a nine iron, like the big boys, when everyone knows the player can't get to the green with a seven iron. And he'll probably shrug when someone curses the placement of a pond. He is the Golf God, not Mother Nature.

For a fleeting moment, I imagine the Golf God, Mother Nature, and the Sun God dining at the top of the CN Tower, overlooking Lake Ontario and making decisions about the next day's weather. Since it's autumn, they'll dine on harvest vegetables, squash, carrots, beans, and roast beef. Mad cow problems don't scare them. And they will sip Ice Wine from the Niagara vineyards, and wrap it up with freshly baked apple crisp. They'll have a fourth as their ad hoc guest. Old Man Winter would be there, smiling, promising a decent winter and looking like a politician during an election run.

Early in the spring, Mother Nature, the Sun God, and the Golf God would dine in Ottawa, on the lawn of the Parliament buildings, counting the budding tulips, indulge on dandelion wine, oysters on the half shell, energising pasta primavera, and chocolate cheesecake with raspberry sauce. Their guest for the evening would be that little whiz kid, Cupid.

"I'm getting old and tired, generating all that solar power." The Sun God would ask for some time off.

Mother Nature will insist. "Some rain to nourish the grass. Some warmth and sunshine to make it grow."

The Golf God requests, "It has to balance out."

Cupid prances around and proclaims, "Love is in the air," and shoot arrows at the idea of accepting any physical responsibility.

"We have to be fiscally responsible," The Golf God would suggest. "Three years ago we had excessive heat. The next year, excessive rain. Last year, a wet cold spring. I just got a new one iron and I need some practice."

"You're saying I've taken off too many vacation days?" The Sun God took offense. "Don't make me angry. I can flare up and mess things up for days at a time. I can flare out and shut down the power grid."

"All we're looking for is some kind of balance to our summers."

"I've got coupons!" Mother Nature said. "I know they are here somewhere. Here! Look. A hundred and sixty days of sunshine. Rain at night."

"That coupon has expired." The Sun God would cross his arms and stare in one direction. "Besides, my costs have gone up. I want a raise." Then he'd pout. "If I can't have a raise, I want more time off, to practice."

"Be nice!" Cupid would shoot an arrow at the Sun God and hit him in the eye. "Oops. Well, you know what they say. Love is blind."

Everyone knows only God can hit a perfect one iron. Why would he need to practice?

Okay, so I'm delirious.

My body feels like wet bread. I have been attacked by a flotilla of tees, bombarded by errant and precisely aimed tee shots, dismissed as a leech and either ignored or attacked by pretty well every golfer at the CrossCreek Golf and Country Club. My only source for an optimistic outcome is that if hell did freeze over and my corpse was frozen in the pond of the 17th hole, I wouldn't have to pay off my golf club bills, the divorce lawyer, nor the bets I lost last weekend.

I didn't want to believe the guys didn't want to collect what I owed them.

It had to be time to pray to the Golf God.

"As I lay me down to sleep, I pray the Golf God, my putter to keep. Give my partners playing rights, birdies, pars and eagles, which they dream of every night. Keep my Pings and MaxFli balls and let my opponents slice with soaring heights, on courses with doglegs only to the right. As I lay me down to sleep, let the Golf God help me see the light."

Kaida whimpered which brought my attention to where he was. He laid down with his chin on his crossed paws. His nose and big brown eyes are pointed right at me.

Chapter 16

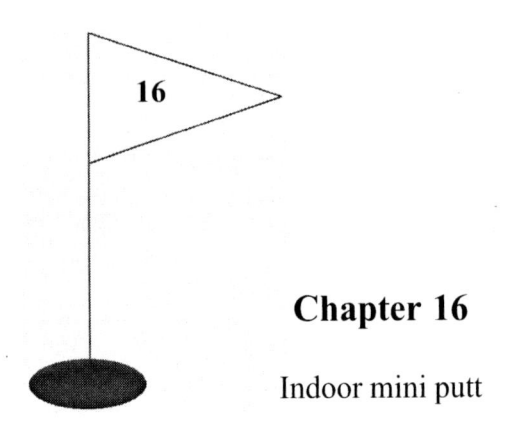

Indoor mini putt

There is no one on the tee. No one glaring down at the green, assessing the distance, and comparing his or her past good or bad shots to the 17th green. Except for Kaida's presence, I'm alone with my thoughts again.

"Kaida. Be a Lassie and go get someone who can help me. There's a good dog. Go on now. Get help."

Kaida lifted his head then sat up. His white chest proud as any hero in the making.

"Big T. Bone in it for you, Kaida. Go get help." I offered the mutt a bribe.

He cocked his head.

"Go get some help. I'm starting to freeze in here. Go on you, mutt."

Kaida growled, barked and snoot in the air marched away. Halfway up the hill he looked back, barked, and trotted off. He's not headed to the clubhouse to get help. He's headed up the cliff-side path to the 17th tee. I know border collies are intelligent, but now he acts as if he took offense that I called him a mutt.

The business ladies, all of the next four foursomes came through the 17th like a gale force wind. I couldn't get them to stop long enough to even think about dragging me out of the pond. Speed demons! Slow down! Enjoy the walk in a park. Someone said golf is a good walk ruined. Well, at the speed the ladies played, who has time to see the scenery?

Alone again.

It's not a situation I especially like. But I've been all wet before now.

Since I'm living on my own, I don't have to go home to a wife and since my apartment is less than perfect, any reason to be at the golf club is good enough for me. The last time I felt this wet was after one of our seriously rich club tournaments.

One of the major tournaments and the last one of the season at our club is the 'Pot of Golf.' It's a betting man's weekend. There is a lot of money on the line that weekend. Players sign up as teams, pick their own foursomes, and play on Saturday as the 'qualifying' round. As the Saturday scores are written on the scoring sheets, the players and teams eye the numbers like stats for the next race at Woodbine Race Track. Then the fun begins.

Bets are laid on the team that will win, your own team and the one you think has the best thoroughbred, the Derby winner, the best tournament players. Bets are placed on win, show, place. Paramutuals. It's a cash only event.

And then the final round of eighteen holes is played the next day, scores are tallied, drinks flow, and bets are paid off. One year over twenty-seven thousand dollars changed hands.

"The Pot of Golf" tournament is played near the end of the season, when the trees are just about to lose their coloured leaves, when the air is crisp and clean, and a lost ball could really be lost or just hiding under a pile of red maple leaves.

That year we played the Saturday round in the rain. It was a day when one of those north winds blustered at the course, making the long holes downwind, and very short because of the wind. As a cross wind it made the longest par-three hole terrific for guys who hit a long slice. But it also had an arctic chill, and the smell of snow behind it. It wasn't the kind of golfing weather I liked, but I dressed in layers to keep warm. And there was no way I would ever miss the biggest betting day of the golfing season.

I studied the players in the group all season, I know who is on their 'A' game, who struggled, who will lay bets just to try to get back what they lost all season. The excitement of the day is unmistakable.

I'm at the course early, work through my warm-up routine on the driving range, hang around the putting green, listen to the guys facing the first tee jitters, listen to the jokes and teasing and pre-game excuses about how bad they will play. And I remember all this when it comes time to place my bets.

A lot of the pre-game excuses the golfers came up with were the usual. 'I've got a cold.' 'My shoulder is sore from cleaning out my eaves.' 'I have a sore neck.' 'I must have slept badly.' 'My wife had guests in last night and I drank too much wine. It's her fault.' 'I had a lesson.' 'My shoes feel tight.' 'My lace broke.' The excuses for the anticipated bad game are endless.

Then there are the pre-game warnings that come spouting forth from every player. 'I've finally figured out what's wrong with my putting stroke, my swing, my tempo.' 'I've just had my clubs re-gripped so you know I'm going to make some good shots.' 'I've had a lesson. I've been chipping, putting, pitching every night this week.' These guys were bragging about how good they are going to be, today.

Watching these guys get ready for the Fall Classic, Pot of Golf, is like watching a corral of thoroughbred racehorses at Woodbine raceway just before the Queen's Plate. Some of the players twitch, stretch, grin, laugh too loud, don't laugh at all, and check for extra balls. The mood around the pro shop and the first tee is loaded with anticipated success and self-fulfilling prophetic failure. They remind me of a salesman about to go on the most important sales call of his life.

It's pretty obvious most of the golfers have never taken the Dale Carnegie salesman's course, and with the kind of money that's on the line, it is obvious they have never played serious poker. None of them can bluff very well. The whites of their eyes are flipping all over inner space.

It was definitely going to be a lucrative weekend for me. Now, to spice up my betting life, I spent most of the week handicapping each player, guessing how he would survive, play, score and if there really is any chance for him to win. Throw in the official tournament handicap as tracked by the club pro, figure out the partnerships and their prior wins and losses and my notes look like a handicapper's horse race sheet.

My wife once told me that if I spent as much time perfecting my job skills, as I do calculating the golfers handicaps, I'd be a CEO by now. She didn't understand that if I was a CEO with my numbers juggling skills, I'd be in the Don Jail, bouncing golf balls off the bars and facing huge fines as ordered by the Ontario Securities Commission.

And if I was a CEO, I'd have to work too many hours just to keep up with all the work. When would I have time to play golf? When would I have time to work out these betting plans? No, I was doing fine as a middle management manager who could leave the office at a decent time and let the CEO's and VP's get away with their own indiscretions. Besides, if I made a larger salary, my taxes would be higher. All the cash I make at the golf course was tax-free. Totally tax-free.

As we wound up our qualifying round for the Fall Classic, Pot of Golf, we drank, eyed the scores, drank some more beer and laid bets. Then we drank as we eyed the bets, and justified, rationalized and bragged about the methods we use to make our bets. We drank some more to celebrate Kevin's low round, Randy's eagle putt, Jack's sand shot. We drank some more and watched rain pelt against the floor to ceiling windows. We drank some more as we watched the creek in front of the eighteenth green suck water from the elevated green. We drank some more as we worried about whether the course would be playable the next day. We even had a moment of silence for our respectful admiration of the Golf God.

None of the die hard drinkers wanted to go out in the rain, run to their cars and drive home in this autumn rain. So to kill a little time, we built an indoor putting course.

We put down chair cushions to create alley ways, tipped chairs over for the legs to act as back stops and used beer glasses from the bar as holes. The bartender, Donny, wasn't too happy about the potential of broken glass and tried to retrieve the beer glasses from the floor. Just as fast as he lifted a beer glass from the floor, someone finished his beverage and laid his glass down as a target.

Donny's only recourse was to stop serving any kind of booze.

My response was to kneel down on the carpet and suggest the guys putt to my hands. A couple of the guys pretended to take a baseball batter's swing and I pretended to duck. I was laughing so hard I fell over and with that they decided on a point system for putting. Five points if they hit my head. Two points if they missed my head and hit my shoulders.

It didn't occur to me until just now, as I'm shivering in the pond on the 17th hole, that I had one hell of a sore head the next day for that final round of that Fall Classic, Pot of Golf. No wonder I played like an idiot.

Which, by the way, was okay, because I didn't bet much on my own team. I bet on the winners. So I still had a very lucrative weekend. If I'd lost, we might have had to remortgage the house. I didn't tell my wife. Sharon wouldn't understand that sometimes you just have to take a risk.

But this current weekend was going to cost me. My golf bag would be ruined, my clubs would need to be re-gripped. My Mizuno shoes would be worse than a homeless man's pair.

Norm Roberts and his wife Edna, Delson Brummel and his wife Irene, are on the 17th tee. All of them are in their sixties and play together regularly. They are easy to recognize even from a distance. Norm is big round man and swings like Arnie Palmer, always falling back after his swing. His profile is a lot like Alfred Hitchcock's. Delson is the opposite. He's tall and skinny, with long arms and long legs. His clubs always seem way too short. He really should have custom clubs made for him but who knows if any club maker can provide the length he needs and now that the maximum length of a club, excluding putters, is only 48 inches, Delson could be out of luck. Seeing the two of them on the men's tee reminds me of an elephant and a giraffe.

Norm's wife, Edna, is a new golfer and he's taught her well about how to keep up pace of play. She doesn't even bother to tee off from the ladies tees up on the cliff of the 17th hole. I know that both she and Irene will come on down to the level fairway, drop a ball on the green side of the pond and hit to the green from there.

I'm not surprised to see an electric cart come down the hill with Edna driving and Irene as the honoured passenger. Irene's high-pitched voice flew ahead of the speeding cart. Edna didn't have a motor vehicle driver's license but put her in a golf cart and she's a speed driver. The cart careened, wobbled and the two ladies shrieked, hung on and laughed. As the cart wobbled off the tarmac path, heading for the pond, I envision them flying off the edge and landing on top of me.

"NO!" I yelled. "Whoa!"

The cart rocked, the ladies screeched and then when the thing came to a stop inches from the rising bank of the pond, they laughed like banshees and giggled like schoolgirls out joyriding in daddy's car.

"Edna! I told you to use the brake going down hill," Norm yelled from his swerving cart. His golf clubs rattled, wagged, bounced in the bag at the back of the cart. Delson hung on with both hands gripped around the windshield frame.

"Edna! Look!" Irene pointed at me while Edna leaned over trying to find the switch on the dash to reverse the cart. Edna looked up over the dash and stared at me.

"Hi, Mrs. Roberts." I gave them my best smile. "Hello, Mrs. Brummel."

"Come on, Edna," Norm yelled from his now stopped cart on the path. "Let's go."

"Norm. Look. It's Michael Blaine." Edna pointed.

"Where? What are you talking about?" Norm hoisted his bulk out of the cart and waddled over to stand beside Edna's cart. He adjusted his glasses and leaned forward. I had a moment of terror that he would fall into the pond and I'll be swallowed by a tidal wave.

"Michael Blaine is in the middle of the pond," Irene said.

"What are you doing in there?" Norm bellowed at me and leaned backwards.

"Oh, you know. Just… sort of swimming." I didn't say I'm swimming in regrets.

"You'll catch your death, swimming in this kind of weather." Irene huddled her windbreaker closer. "You should get out of there, Michael."

"That's probably a good idea, Mrs. Brummel. But you see, the guys are pulling a stunt. You know, they tied me to my golf bag and threw me in."

"You're stuck in there?" Edna asked. Her hands gripped the steering wheel. The look on her face was like road rage took over. Then the cart jerked backwards and looped around so now I could see their golf bags on the back of the cart.

"You want us to throw you a rope?" Delson called to me.

"Well. Sure, but I really am tied to my golf bag."

"Does your wife know you're in there?" Edna asked and blinked.

"Edna. They split up. He's been dating Melanie," Irene said.

"What! Michael, is that true?" By now Edna was standing at the edge of the pond, hands on her hips and a serious scowl on her face.

"Well? That's not entirely true," I said. "Not really."

"You left your wife for another woman?" Edna yelled.

"We had a mutual falling out, Edna."

She harrumphed and snorted, then turned and started to dig in her golf bag.

"Come on, Edna, let's go." Norm headed back to his cart.

"We'll come back out with a rope or something, Michael." Delson waved over his shoulder.

"Thanks, Mr. Brummel. I'd appreciate that."

The splash dotted my face with pond water and when I looked at the source, Edna was throwing a golf ball at me. That one was wide.

"Ah, Mrs. Roberts?"

"You shouldn't have left your wife, Michael." She lobbed another ball at me.

"Edna!" Norm waddled toward her. "You throw like a girl. How many times have I taught you how to throw a ball?"

"It's too small. I can't get a good grip on it." She lost control of another golf ball and it flopped about five feet in front of her. Norm picked a ball out of her bag, placed it in her hand and I couldn't hear how he coached her, but the next ball whizzed past my right ear.

"Mrs. Roberts!" I pleaded. "NORM!"

Another one came at me, right for my forehead. I ducked and the ball skimmed off the top of my head. I came up spluttering water and yelled at them. "What's that for?"

"For your wife. You no good kitten kicker!"

"You tell him, Edna," Irene yelled.

"Norm?" I screamed.

"Don't look at me. You still owe me twenty bucks from last weekend."

"Come on, you guys," Delson called. "Let's go. If we don't hurry up, we'll get a letter for slow play, again! Let's go."

Norm lunged into Edna's cart and drove away, leaving Edna to glare at me. My salvation is only because she's out of ammunition. She started marching and pointed at me as she rounded the end of the pond. As I watched her leave me, I have to agree with Sir Winston when he said, 'There is nothing more exhilarating than being shot at but without result.'

I didn't win that battle but I was labelled as a... a kitten kicker? I suppose that could be better than being the new Ontario Premier, Liberal Dalton McGuinty who was accused by the Conservatives, in an accidentally released memo, as a 'kitten eater.' Hell, he'd won the election, so if I'm a kitten kicker, is that a good thing? Or a bad thing? I sure hope the new honourable Provincial Premier, kitten eater or not, follows through on his election platform promise and improves the healthcare in the province.

If I don't get out of this pond soon, I'm going to need health care, for frostbite.

Chapter 17

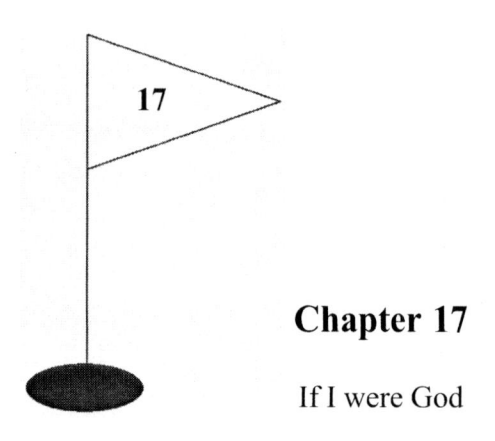

If I were God

My hopes are sinking. So far, I can't convince the guys I normally play with to haul me out of the pond on the 17th hole on this glorious autumn day. I had avoided some of them, called out to others but all to no avail. When the business ladies started coming around to the 17th tee, I tried my luck begging for their help but much to my disappointment, some of them were married to my so-called golfing buddies and weren't very appreciative of my solicitous ways. Some of the business ladies took Melanie's side. Some are just plain full-grown cat eaters. Even Freud admitted that he didn't understand what women want. I begged. I asked nicely. I made some promises. In the past I had taught some of them sand shots, how to make get-out-of-jail shots, how to hit a slice on command. Today I thought about bribing them, but I was reluctant to even try that. According to Mother, women are a lot more ethical than men.

Maybe like Edna, I needed a better grip, or at the very least a bigger ball to grip. I guess it's time to consider my blessings.

It is a glorious day. The sky is bluer than Calgary boasts. The sun is as clear and as bright as a polished gold nugget. The weeds on the side of the cliff are shrinking and turning brown. The wild flowers are in their final bloom. The willow tree drapes branches tipped with blonde tresses that shift in the breeze like a California beach surfer-girl. The bulrushes haven't yet finished for the season, haven't yet turned to fluff. The water lilies are pushing out their final pink and rose red colours. The row of pines that hide the greenskeeper's sheds are a spectacular emerald green backdrop for the border of brilliant red leaves of the Sumac bushes. Blue jays bounce on the slight branches of the red berry laden Mountain Ash trees. All in all, it is a beautiful October day.

I wished the Blue Jays baseball team had bounced back as easily as the blue-coated birds bounce around the branches. That game when one player hit four homers in one game was something. Spirits had been recharged. What a high that was for all the local baseball fans. Since the Blue Jays aren't in the World Series, ball fans were hoping for a Boston Red Sox versus Cubs historic ending to the baseball season. But I bet on the Florida Marlins against the New York Yankees. I am a golfer and I love warm weather. Florida is the place to be.

It wasn't good news about the CFL having to take over the Hamilton TiCats football team because someone mucked about with the funding. But maybe this year would be the Argos year and we'll have a Grey Cup to remember. And maybe the Toronto Maple Leafs, our hockey heroes of forty years ago, can, this year, pull a rabbit out of the hat and go all the way to the Stanley Cup winner's circle.

Who am I kidding? The Leafs? Yeah, right. But hope runs eternal. I'd still bet on the Leafs for every game of their season. I am a die-hard Toronto Maple Leafs fan. That is, if I don't die in this pond on the 17th hole of CrossCreek Golf and Country Club.

For all the glory of the day, for all the bright sunshine and brilliant autumn colours, my season is fading very fast. Afternoon sun, though brilliant, is losing its warmth.

I'm not religious like Al Kazan. I'm not as honest as Rick Kirkwood, Mr. Revenue Canada. I've made a mockery of my marriage vows. My career is swirling down a familiar path. The economy is leaking. The stock market is in a bear market, snoring and snuggling into hibernation. Every day another CEO lands in jail. I am thinking about all this and wondering if I committed to the correct fork in the road, the honest route to redemption, will anyone believe me?

Will anyone miss me if I just put my face in the water and try to breathe like a fish? If God had wanted me to be a fish, he would have made me a fish. I am not a fish. I am a sandbagger. I purposely keep my handicap high. I don't enter my low scores in the computer for tracking. I'm a tournament golfer. I play better if money is on the line. I'm addicted to making a bet.

I don't gamble at casinos, don't play poker very often, but I gamble with other aspects of my life. My wife accuses me of tailgating, driving too fast, and drinking too much. Playing the stock market, procrastinating at work. There are a slew of things I'm obviously doing wrong.

"Hey, Mikey, I got a joke for you."

I was lost in my regrets and didn't see Ivan approach. So when I looked up from my reflected face in the pond, Ivan Miller, a man who seldom remembers a joke, usually forgot the punch line or stuttered as he stood up to relate some story he thought was amusing, I almost groaned out loud. He is a nice guy but a lousy joke teller.

"Ivan, I have enough troubles right now."

He made no mention of the fact that I was up to my chin in pond water. "Ya gotta hear this one, Mikey. This one is made for you. Besides, where are you going to go? I got me a captive audience."

Ivan cleared his throat, took a deep breath and started.

"Four guys had finished putting on the 17th hole." Ivan pointed at the green then turns and points at the cliff. "Up on the 17th tee, there's a guy standing there like some prophet on the mountain. 'He looks like Moses,' one guy says.

"So the man on the tee, he tees off and his ball goes into the pond." Ivan starts to move like he's the hero of his joke. "He walks down and parts the waters, finds his ball and a dozen others. He takes out a lob wedge and hits his ball to the green.

"A second guy tees off and his ball goes into the pond. He walks down, walks on the water and picks out his ball. Sets it on the surface, hits it into the hole.

"One of the guys in the group behind them, watching all this, says, 'Who does he think he is? Jesus Christ? Moses? God?'

"So the other guy says, you're gonna love this, Mikey. The other guy says, 'If he was God, he'd put it in the hole the first time.'"

"Good one, Ivan. Really good. Thanks," I said.

"I knew you'd like that one. Seeing as how you're in the pond." Ivan laughed and walked to the green.

I am alone again, with my regrets. My body temperature has dropped and my enthusiasm for the game is quickly waning. I check off names of the guys I normally play golf with and who will probably never play with me again. I will probably have to quit this course and find another place to play golf. Then again, maybe this is my final opportunity to give up the game and fly right. Maybe if I had put as much effort into my relationship with my wife and marriage as I do to my hustling and golf handicapping, I'd still be living with my wife, enjoying her homemade chili, her laughter, her sympathetic ear and the way the sun has highlighted her hair. I deeply regretted our roaring departure, which was like both of us riding on two muffler-less Harley Davidsons heading in opposite directions.

If I were God I'd design less sadistic golf courses, golf balls that float, tees that are made out of turf fertiliser and wild flower seeds. I'd devise grudges that melt quickly, and angry words that come with mufflers.

Chapter 18

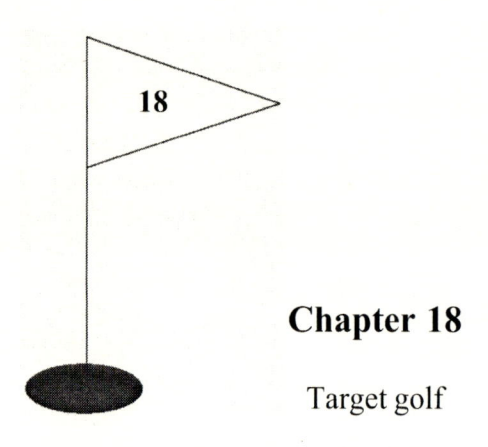

Target golf

As the sun tries to hide behind the willow to my left, casting pointing shadow fingers at the cliff that is the teeing area of the 17th hole, I deliriously eye the patterns on the surface of the pond. In search of some symbolic gesture, or pattern to the dark water glassy top, I hope that a form of redemption appears. All I see is the reflection of the maple leaves, blood red smearing against the murky brown of my reflected image.

When the leaves turn vibrant autumn colours, as the arctic chill snakes its way down from Yellowknife, passionate golfers all over southern Ontario lament for just one more warm day. Every day for the months of September and October, golfers I know beseech the golf god for one more day. One more chance to hit the three hundred yard drive straight down the middle of the fairway, the opportunity to eagle that par five, the prospect to sink that downhill left to right breaking thirty foot putt for par, and even better, the justification to celebrate a hole-in-one. At that moment, I'd be happy to be in the clubhouse celebrating Al Kazan's hole-in-one.

Some Ontario golfers I know head to the southern climes of the Niagara peninsula to extend their golf season. Some courses in that area are open twelve months of the year. Some golfers play in a golf tournament on the day after Christmas, rain or shine, snow or frost. There is no explanation for the passion that that straight drive, that long putt, that flawless lob shot, that exquisite bunker shot causes in the hearts of all golfers. Young, old, beginners and experts luxuriate in the thrill of a finely executed shot. Some say it's better than sex.

In the past, as winter rolled into the Great Lakes region, I yearned for a longer golfing season, a better year, and a hole-in-one. As golfers depart the course to spend another winter wishing for longer summers in Ontario, we calm each other's groans about a bad scoring season by saying, "There's always next year." I always hoped to be a participant next year, planned to improve my putting, control my slice, and improve my net worth, but now I just hope to survive today.

There hasn't been a golfer on the tee in a long time but maybe as one contemplates the end, time moves at a slower pace. Perhaps as one's body temperature decreases, as hypothermia sets in, the flow of blood decelerates and thoughts are harder to form and sounds are muffled. I no longer yearn for a longer golfing season: I am pinned down, alone on a water lily decorated death row, and waiting for the cyanide pellet to drop. It's time to review my accomplishments.

I have never made a shot like Tiger Woods did at the Canadian Open in 2002, from the sand 160 yards out on the 18th hole at Glen Abbey and I probably never will make a spectacular shot like that. I have never made a hole-in-one, ever, but I was there to witness my father's 190-yard shot during a tournament at Lakeview Course in Mississauga. I have never been to Augusta to watch the Masters Tournament, but I prayed for Mike Weir to win it in April 2003 and the golf gods must have been listening to Canadians that day.

Now, I wondered what I'd have to do to appease the golf gods.

CrossCreek Golf and Country Club has a stable of electric carts that move without engine noise. The carts are so quiet that in the spring, you can hear the frogs singing in the ponds calling out for compatible mates, the hum and buzz of wasp wings flitting above empty pop cans in the trash bins, a strong breeze whistling through the fescue and the delicious sound of your opponent's ball plopping into a distant pond. So quiet are the golf carts that you'd think they were ghost ships.

I heard that sound, that plopping noise and looked around me for the source of the ripples. I stared up at the cliff and saw absolutely no one, but I did see another ball flying in my direction. It landed short of the pond and disappeared without a bounce in the long lush grass. Then another flying spot came over the ridge and that one landed at the end of the pond to my left. The water lilies shook as the surface reverberates with two more plopping golf balls. The shots are coming faster than a machine gun.

"HEY!" I yelled. "Hey!"

Then I saw the line of human forms approach the cliff. My father was a fan of Westerns and he'd actually groan out loud when the line of Comanches appeared in ambush mode along the ridge as the heroes of the story rode through the canyon. As I watched the dozen or so golfers armed with short irons, take positions like a chorus line of hyped up Comanches, I can't control the groan that erupted out of my chest. They are all going to hit shots at the same time. I have no choice but to bury my head in the pond and hope the hard as rocks hail of golf balls doesn't actually hit me.

I sincerely wish that George, my biker buddy, had offered me his Harley helmet.

The dozen plopping golf balls resounded through the water, and I was, so far, unscathed, but I had to come up for air. I watched the water lilies shudder with shock waves and then eyed the shadowy villains on the cliff.

"Come on, you guys. Haul me out of here. This isn't funny any more," I yelled up at them.

Then they came marching down the tarmac path, some carrying their golf bags, some dragging carts. They were so close together, in the shadow of the cliff that it looked like a herd of mustangs staggering down the path. A new line of shooters formed at the top of the cliff. By their shapes and profiles I know this group is made up of the business ladies. I count eight of them. They all swung in synchronised moves and eight golf balls soared into the sky, one flying longer and farther. One golfer hooted and cheered as the other seven balls plunked into the pond. The water lilies destroyed by the pot shot holes. The surface rocked with ripples.

"What'd I do to you?" I yelled up at the ladies, but the marching row of men were forming a firing squad line-up in front of me, not twenty feet from the edge of the pond.

"Remember, men. We want a low flyer this time. Line drive. Use your 'get out of jail' shot."

"Whoa! Hold it!" I screeched. "I'm the one in jail. Get me out!"

"Choose your weapons!" Pear shaped Philip Perry in Napoleon's pose, stood with one hand pressed against his belly and one arm raised up holding a metal wood like a sword. His body was weaving back and forth like he'd swallowed too much of Napoleon's brandy. Golfers pulled irons from their bags and some tossed golf balls up in the air like a set of jugglers.

"Wait, Philip! Don't I even get a trial? You've jumped right to the firing squad."

"At ease, men," Philip yelled and with Chi Chi Rodrigues's trademark move, slid his sword-club into an imaginary scabbard at his hip. He marched to the edge of the pond and rocked back on his heels.

A golf ball landed in the pond right in front of him and he turned and yelled up at the cliff, and crossed the air with an arm. "Cut that out," he yelled up at the ladies.

I heard tires on the gravel pathway and aimed my stare toward the hill near the greenskeeper's sheds. A line of electric golf carts came down the slope from the pro shop like a line of Hell's Angels bikers. I swear I heard Harley motors.

"Edna got a hole-in-one!" someone yelled from the cliff, and the ladies started hooting and trucking down the hill.

"You were supposed to aim for the pond!" Norm yelled up to the cliff.

"All right, Edna!" I bellowed. "Way to go!"

Then the carts, each carrying a pair of golfers, the firing squad, and the business ladies who had joined them at the edge of the pond stared down at me.

"I think you should use putters," Irene Brummel said. "Or drivers like Tiger putts from the edge of the green. Wouldn't you have better aim?"

"Irene!" I called to her. "Irene. It's me, Mikey. Why are you coaching them?"

"I know about you. I know what you did. Now hold still."

"Putters, everyone!" Philip yelled, pulled out his driver and waved it around like a sword.

I could pick out Manni, the Godfather, who stood back to one side, and beside him stood the very Christian Al Kazan, sipping from a beer glass. They are an odd pairing. Then I spotted Al Compton, and Frank Craig helping blind Bob Murtiss line up his shot.

And Jeff, the lawyer, now with his shirttail hanging out and wobbling as he leaned on his putter, definitely looked three sheets to the wind. "Ya gotta pay the penalty, Mikey," Jeff slurred, rocked back and forth, almost fell back too far, but there right behind him was Jimmy, Ken and Dan, to hold him up. The three of them needed each other just to stay upright themselves. Being the first ones off the course they'd been in the bar over three hours. Knowing those three, they were probably celebrating royally at how they had worked all day to weigh down my golf bag and then tacked me off the cart path on the 17th hole, wrapped straps around my arms and tied me to the golf cart. Then like hauling a massive log, they'd swung me back and forth and tossed me into the water. They're so drunk now, Jimmy's eyes are crossed. Ken's hair stands straight up and Dan is trying to hit on Edna. They're blind drunk but, so far, as I can tell the rest of the firing squad, except for Bob Murtiss, aren't. And since Bob wouldn't be driving a car home, he's the only one who really should be the designated drunk.

I have to think fast. I have to defend myself. "Guys, guys! Remember that night I was the designated drunk, and distracted the cops so all you guys could get home without a ticket. I never asked you guys to help me pay the fine."

"We've all assumed that persona, as the designated decoy drunk, on at least one occasion," Dr. Neville Decorte, the psychotherapist, pointed out.

"Heh, heh, overruled!" Jeff declared, waved his club in the air and fell over. Three guys pulled him up and pushed his wobbling form against the front bumper of a golf cart. Jeff thumped his club against the cart, like a gavel. "I'm the judge. Next!"

Kathy Regan, one of the business ladies, slumped beside Jeff. "I'm a judge, too."

"Gotta have three," I said and quickly added, "I want Manni."

"Manni's the superior court judge, and in this case, your worst case appellate court," someone yelled.

"Then I want Al Kazan." I figured a good Christian oriented gentleman would be on my side.

"Hang 'em," Al yelled as he marched over to the golf cart.

"Al, remember how I drove all the juniors to the Accuform tournament that time you couldn't go? Al?" While he pondered that I spotted Ivan, the worst joke teller at the club. "Ivan! Remember how we rehearsed that joke before you had to make that speech at that tournament? Remember we worked on that for hours?"

"You really helped me with that, Mikey." Ivan nodded vigorously then fell over like a tree toppling in the forest. The two members on either side of him stood there like owls in a tree, staring down at him, but no one made a move to help him up.

"George?" I called out to the native Indian gospel singer that nearly gave Al a heart attack. "George, remember the time you called from jail and needed bail money?"

"Overruled!" Kathy yelled. "I paid you back for that."

"It was two in the morning!" I yelped back at her.

"Choose your weapons," Philip yelled. "Putters! HO!"

"Jeff! Remember how I helped you retrieve your wife's electric cart from the pond? Melanie, what about how I gave you sandtrap lessons? Aren't you the best bunker player in your group? Norm, remember the business plan I drafted for you? Didn't it help you get that business loan? Peter—"

The roar of a Harley Davidson growled from the near distance. It thundered like an angry herd of Sabre toothed tigers coming at us from the echoes of an ice age. The unmistakable growl and throbbing rumble of a finely tuned road hog punctured the silence. It had to be George Warburton. I hoped he was the Lone Ranger, coming to rescue me from this firing squad. Putters at twenty yards would be deadly.

Running along beside the Harley was Kaida, barking and bounding over the weeds.

George Warburton is still dressed in black, but it's shiny leather with silver studs at the seams and everyone one of those studs shot back sunlight like machine gun fire. On his head is a huge black helmet with a dark and reflective facemask that I hope is hiding a grin. A rescuer's grin.

The line of golfers parted like the Red Sea as the Harley cruised up the middle, the front wheel almost filling my view. He revved the motor, rocked the bike forward and I expected it to rear up like Hi HO Silver!

"GEORGE!" I rocked like an excited puppy. Water lapped and rippled away from me like a tidal wave in early creation.

Kaida barked and like a homeless drunk looking for a handout, nosed each member of the jury. He licked faces of the fallen drunks with no result.

A second helmet appeared beside George Warburton's and I studied this new recruit closely. When she climbed off the bike, her curves clung to the black leather outfit. She was a slim, long legged goddess in leather, with a jacket that sported fringe from wrists to elbows. She strutted to the edge of the pond and stood with fists on her hips, legs apart and so far, because of the helmet and lowered face guard, she's unrecognisable. She looked over her shoulder at the biker and the rumbling sound quit.

I have a vague notion that I know the woman in leathers. Her shape is familiar, but I'm absolutely certain that George Warburton has never introduced me to his girlfriend. He has been very secretive lately.

She shifted her position and stood staring at me with her arms folded across her chest, the fringe on the sleeves hanging down like a short skirt. Then she spread her arms, the fringe looked like wings of an eagle and the silence that followed became more ominous than the row of armed golfers.

"Can I add to the charges?" she asked from inside the helmet. The sound was a little like Darth Vader. Or maybe that mechanical heavy breathing sound is my chest trying to deny this unwelcome intruder.

The sound is familiar, like when someone yells at you while you're in the shower.

My wife! Soon to be ex-wife!

"George! What have you done?" I whimpered. "George! You're dating my wife?"

George Warburton walked toward me, sauntered like he owned the place. He stopped momentarily at the edge of the pond.

"Manni!" I have to use my trump card. "Manni! Remember that afternoon when I was shooting the best game of my life, but you blew out a kneecap and we had to call an ambulance! Manni! Remember I went with you to the hospital? Called your wife. Manni?"

"Hang on a second, George." Manni stepped up to the edge of the pond and they formed a conspiring triangle. I'm going to have to come up with something better than all the things I've done for the golfers at this club. I have to make a final appeal to my wife.

"Sharon, sweetheart. Remember that time I hauled your brother out of the drunk tank, took him to the AA meetings?"

She pulled off the helmet and squinted at me, waiting for more.

"Remember I even lied to your mother so she wouldn't know he was a drunk? Remember the alibi I used to give him, so no one but us knew he went to AA? Remember that? Sharon? Sweetheart? Remember how I took your mother with us on that holiday to Hawaii? Sharon? Two weeks, Sharon, with your mother on our vacation? Remember that?"

The silence was deafening. Really spooky. The sun was behind trees and long shadows touched the bodies of the firing squad. Only their bodies are in shadows, with spotlights on their faces, and all of them are holding up their putters looking like ghostly rows of armed and dangerous.... Sword bearing attackers.

"Sharon?" I had to convince her. At that moment she appears to be the only sober one of the bunch. Two more members dropped to the ground and those still standing are swaying like a willow tree branches in a wind.

"Sharon? Remember what Shakespeare said about love? A madness most discreet and when vexed, is a sea nourished by a lover's tears."

"I like what Lennon said," she said from the trio at the edge of the pond. "Love is like a precious plant. You can't leave it in the cupboard. You have to water it."

"You did this to me? You arranged this?"

"Had enough water yet, Mikey?"

"Sharon? YOU?" I'm stunned. As if the pond had suddenly become a hockey rink, squeezing against my chest, freezing my lungs, my chest iced up.

Then Sharon handed her helmet to George Warburton. She said something to him and then he turned and stepped into the pond. He walked through the water, dragging her helmet along the surface. The water touched his chest, a slight wake flowed out from behind him and he kept coming.

"George, what can I say?" I was desperate. "George?"

"Afraid you're doomed, Michael." George then scooped water into Sharon's helmet and poured the whole lot over my head. As I spluttered water from my mouth, he pushed the helmet down over my ears. The facemask was still up.

"Wait! What can I do?" I waited and he peered into my eyes as if to find some truth in my pupils. I hope he'll see the mark of fear.

He flipped down the plexiglass facemask.

"George. Wait! I'll…" My voice echoed inside the helmet and I watched through the tinted plexi as George turned and wadded back to the edge. Manni and George Campbell pulled George Warburton from the pond, then Sharon, Manni and the two Georges manhandled Bob Murtiss and lined him up to take a shot at me. Then they stepped to the side. The only movement now is George Warburton shaking a leg like Kaida did after the mutt fell into the pond.

All faces turned toward Sharon.

Then Sharon nodded.

Philip raised his driver-sword. "Ready! Aim!"

"Wait! I'll change," I screamed. "Sharon, I never wanted a divorce!"

"Fire!"

Bang, plunk, plop, bang-bang-bang. The balls came at me too fast for me to duck. Golf balls caromed off the helmet, the plexi facemask, and my shoulders. The machine gun rapid fire stopped and I looked up. The squad has moved closer to the edge of the pond. They're ready to hit another batch of golf balls at me.

"Wait! I haven't given you the year-end financial report. I'm not the big winner this year. I have all the stats. I can prove I'm not the big winner. I have… all the stats. Jack, you never touched a flag all year. Billy, you never missed a sand save. Norm, you had the least number of putts all year. Manni, blowing your kneecap fixed your swing. George, that fund-raising pancake breakfast at your church. I was there flipping flapjacks, Al, the time I drove your mother to the hospital. Doesn't any of that stuff count? Doesn't any of that soften your hearts? Sharon? Sweetheart?"

Bob Murtiss, the blind golfer, is still trying to line up his shot, held a cupped hand to his ear, the palm open to my sound bites. He's checking for me on his radarscope.

"Okay. Okay. Wait!" I bellowed again.

"I got a line on him now." Bob shifted his shoulders.

"Bob, wait. Hold on a second. Bob, you'll miss me if you take your shot now. Your shoulders aren't straight, Bob." He adjusted his grip and his stance.

"Now take your best shot, Bob. Wait! Wait! Here's the deal. If he hits me, you all have to pull me out. See! I lined him up. He's got a dead-on aim this time." I rocked my head showing them that I was willing to move as much as I could to take a hit.

From what I can tell, my offer to be the bull's-eye isn't sinking into their collective consciousness. Reaction times from the inebriated semi-conscious does take longer.

"What's going on? Can I take a shot or not?" Bob asked.

"What if I promise never to play golf again? I'll take the twelve step program!" I yelled.

"Ah shit!" Philip lowered his raised sword like weapon.

One by one, they marched past me like mourners at a funeral service, viewing the open casket.

"KAIDA.A.A!" I bellowed.

Chapter 19

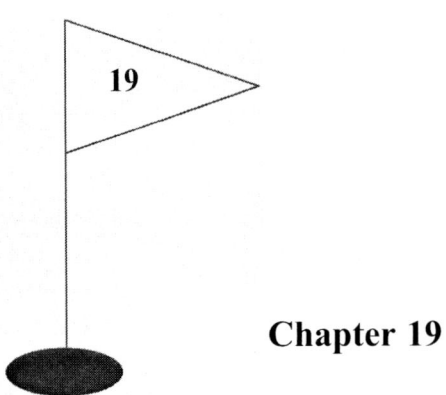

Welcome to the 19th hole.
My name is Michael. And I am a sandbagger.

It's true what they say. You never really want to climb out of the gutter until you hit rock bottom. For an alcoholic, he, or she, can be in a fog so long that he doesn't even realize he has hit the bottom of the keg. No matter what he does, until he recognises there is a problem, he doesn't even want to attempt to climb out.

For me, I had lost my job, my wife, my house, my girlfriend, my playing partners and worse, I'd lost my betting opponents. I had nowhere to go but down. But my golfcart wheels were mired in mud and I was hooked on to it high enough to keep my face out of the water. Like ducking my responsibilities, I ducked whenever a golfer took aim.

I even had the arrogance to advise a target shooter that his or her alignment was off kilter and he would miss me. I'd lay bets they'd miss. When I dodged a skipping ball that came at me like a flat stone tossed on a shimmering Muskoka lake, they told me to hold still.

Conceited as I was, I pointed out the errors that they had made. I listed the things I had done for them hoping that these would speak for me.

As judgmental as they were of my actions, I bounced back their secret mistakes and netted the embarrassment of the accused.

Totally unaccustomed to the concept of asking for permission, I begged for forgiveness.

When none of that worked and I contemplated spending the winter with the pond frozen around me, I began to make promises.

At first the mourners continued their slow march away, but as my voice became louder, stronger, they paused and then they turned as if a bus full of passengers had slowed for an accident at the side of the road. Then they came back and stood at the north side of the pond. The autumn sun was low in the sky and lighted their faces like individual performers, like a set of actors on a stage about to take their final bow. But they waited.

"I learned my lesson." I said. "I'll take the twelve step program! In my waterlogged Mizuno shoes, I promise on my Scottsdale, Arizona, Ping putter, I pledge on my 18 carat gold divot repair tool…

"No more psycho psych out games,

No more handicapping the players for the para-mutual betting,

No more tournament play,

No more alibis from the pro shop,

No more debts to pay, or collect,

No more grounding my club in a bunker or hazard,

No more coaching with incorrect advice,

No more than 14 clubs in my bag,

No more kicking the ball from behind a tree,

No more pressing bets on the 18th hole, in fact, no more betting on the golf course at all,

No more entering the wrong score in the computer handicap data bank."

Their silence was punctuated only by the occasional burp or the thud as another drunk golfer fell.

I had to deliver the final act of redemption. The one thing they all needed and only I could provide. I had to take ownership.

"Okay. Okay. I'll be on the handicap committee!"

"Can I take my shot now?" Bob Murtiss bellowed.

"Take your shot, Bob," George Warburton said. "Mikey, if he hits you, we'll haul you out."

I desperately wanted out of the pond.

"Bob? Mr. Murtiss?" I asked with my most charming tone. Inside the helmet it resounded like a gurgle.

"Yeah, Mikey?" Bob aimed his face in my direction.

The silence around the event was interrupted by a thud that came from where the three judges had been propped up by the golf cart. Two of them were standing but peering down at their feet. Manni had disappeared from my view.

'What's going on? Can I hit now or what?" Bob called out.

"It's okay. Manni's drunk and passed out. Go ahead, Bob. Mikey, make sure he hits you or you'll stay there all night," my wife said clearly and I knew she meant it. Sharon usually always means what she says. She seldom lies. Always followed through on threats. She had threatened a divorce and started to follow through on that.

"Okay, Bob. If I talk real even, can you get a radar-read on me? To me it looks like you're aiming way left. Move your left foot forward a bit."

"I got it," Bob said and swung his putter. A mighty whack sounded and the ball skittered above the blades of grass, skipped on the pond surface once, twice, and then veered off to my left and dove like a submarine. I can't move that far to be a direct hit.

"Your other left," I called out to Bob. "Best two out of three shots?" I begged of the crowd.

"I can do it. Give me another shot," Bob whined.

George Warburton helped Manni into the cart then went to Bob and stood behind him. His face rocked, his feet shuffled. He stared down at Bob's golf ball, the putter, adjusted Bob's shoulders and stepped back. "You ready, Mikey?"

"Yeah. Let's do it."

The ball came straight at me, started skipping like a flat stone. I wasn't sure that I could bear to see a ball smash into the facemask, but I had to make sure he hit me. The ball hit the facemask and the sound reverberated inside the helmet like a canon going off.

"Some of the lucky ones snap out it or some life changing Omnipotent Being forces the correction. In my case, it was forced confinement in the pond on the 17th hole at CrossCreek Golf and Country Club. I should have known the winds of change were imminent. I should have known that the golf god had a change of heart about me. I should have recognized that the team in the sky, those Omnipotent Beings, were targeting me. It's easy to say now, since the issue was so clearly brought to my attention, but I really should have recognized the signs that I was an addict.

"So I wear this lapel pin, a little like a battlefield medal," I said to the Sandbaggers Anonymous Group. "I wear it all the time as a reminder. You'll recognize me. I'm the one with waterlogged shoes, waterlilies clinging to my golf bag, bulrushes waving like a flag out of the top of my golf bag. I'm the one wearing the bright and shiny lapel pin that announces my passion and on top of my head is the florescent orange 'Sandbagger!' baseball cap.

"Some people say that smoking is like long-term planning to commit suicide. I quit smoking when I was a sixteen-year-old junior golfer. I will confess that being a fully committed sandbagger is much like long-term smoking." I finished my speech.

As I watched the group who have listened to this tale of woe, as I wait for them to ask for clarification, I make one more pledge, silently. I will never again join a golf course with ponds.

"Any questions?" I asked of the group.

The faces of the group were frozen in time and staring up at me. They are all ages, sizes, and shapes. Some are controlling the urge to ask another question by fidgeting. Some are fiddling with a tee, or a divot repair tool.

A woman waved a hand and asked, "You could have died in that pond. Those three guys who dumped you in there, did they ever get punished?"

"Apparently they were the hired guns to do the dirty job. Everyone was in on it."

One man had a golf ball in his hand, squeezing it like it was one of those tension relievers. Like flags of truce, two putters came up into the air. I pointed to one middle-aged man with a raised putter.

He asked, "So how did you get out of the pond? I mean, did they drain the pond?"

"Unfortunately, I can't tell you that. The greenskeeper made me take a vow never to reveal the tricks of his trade."

"Like a magician can't tell how he creates illusions?" one attendee said.

"Exactly. After all, don't you find the work of the greenskeeping staff extremely mystifying?" I replied.

"Oh yeah. Why do they poke holes in a perfectly good green?" another asked.

"Why do they put sandtraps right where my drive lands? What good is a fairway bunker, anyway?" a woman whined.

"Forget that. What about the tree in the middle of the fairway?" The tee-fiddler held up his four-inch tee.

"And flags right in the middle of a forty-five degree slope on the green?" The person with the Zebra putter waved the club in the air.

"They are sadistic!" That received a massive cheer. "Shoot them all."

I held up my hands to calm the rioting crowd.

The man who has been squeezing a golf ball raised his hand. I nodded to him.

He stood up and asked, "So you're telling us that all you had to do was agree to those twelve things and that stopped the shootout?"

"He said he'd be on the handicap committee."

"Doesn't that give you an easier way to cheat?" one woman asked.

"It's a committee. If he cheated it would be like collusion."

"Exactly," I said.

"So that was it? Then they pulled you out of the pond?'

"Well, that and something my wife said." I paused for effect. "She said that she didn't want me to die in that pond on the 17th hole. She said that when I was a player, at least I came home at night. Then she said…"

This part always breaks me up.

I took a deep breath and finally, I had to wipe a tear from my eye. I held my head up and said to the group, "She said she didn't really mind being a golf widow, but she definitely didn't want to be a real widow."

My name is Michael and I am a Sandbagger.

Epilogue

I'm Michael Blaine, an independent consultant, and now make more with my speaking engagements than I ever did working for an 'ethically' sound company. I'm the founder and executive director of Canadian Sandbaggers Anonymous, which is an enormously profitable corporation, thanks to franchise fees, membership fees, sales of Sandbagger caps, lapel pins, trophies, and calculators designed specifically to manage golf scores and handicap your golfing opponents. I'm available for conferences, tournaments and, for an extra fee, I'll bring Kaida. If you haven't paid your dues, please talk to my wife, Sharon.

For more details see our Website:
www.CanSandbagAnon@pond.org

-The End-